## GIRAFFE

The calf nestled against the adult giraffe, trying to shelter underneath her. But with her forelegs splayed the mother was too low, and the calf had to stand to one side of her instead. He flicked his tail, snorted softly and then began to nudge his mother – almost as if he were trying to help her get up, Mandy thought. But all his mother could do was turn her neck back to lick and nuzzle her baby.

Mandy desperately wished she could do something to save the pair. She willed the calf to run off, to find the herd and safety amongst others. But he remained snuggled against his mother. Like hers, his fate was sealed.

## Animal Ark series

LUCY DANIELS

# Giraffe
## — *in a* —
# Jam

*Illustrations by Ann Baum*

*Hodder
Children's
Books*

a division of Hodder Headline

**Special thanks to Andrea Abbott**
**Thanks also to C. J. Hall, B.Vet.Med., M.R.C.V.S., for reviewing**
**the veterinary information contained in this book.**

Animal Ark is a trademark of Working Partners Limited
Text copyright © 2000 Working Partners Limited
Created by Working Partners Limited, London W6 0QT
Original series created by Ben M. Baglio
Illustrations copyright © 2000 Ann Baum

First published in Great Britain in 2000
by Hodder Children's Books

A Catalogue record for this book is available from the British Library

ISBN 0 340 77845 8

Typeset by Avon Dataset Ltd, Bidford-on-Avon, Warks

Printed and bound in Great Britain by
Clays Ltd, St Ives plc

Hodder Children's Books
a division of Hodder Headline
338 Euston Road
London NW1 3BH

# *One*

'James! Over there!' Mandy Hope whispered, pointing to some bushes to her right, not far from the side of the road.

'Where?' asked her best friend, James Hunter. He leaned across the back seat of the Land-rover and raised his binoculars to his eyes.

'There – in those low bushes – next to that anthill. I think it's a genet,' replied Mandy, still pointing as they moved slowly along the track. 'Can you see it?'

James stared through his binoculars. After a moment he said, 'No. I can only see the bushes and the anthill. Are you sure you saw something?'

'I'm certain. There's a spotted cat in there with a long tail. It's just very well camouflaged.' Mandy explained. 'Remember what Levina told us – don't look *at* the bush. Try to look *through* it – and then you'll see it. Can *you* see it, Levina?'

Dr Levina Lemiso brought the Land-rover to a halt. She gazed through her binoculars towards the bushes.

'Yes, you're right,' agreed Levina. 'I can see a ringed tail. It's a large-spotted genet. It's nocturnal so will probably lie amongst those bushes for the rest of the day. At sunset, it'll start foraging for food.'

Mandy ticked 'large-spotted genet' on the game-sighting list she had picked up at the reception desk at Ubungane Lodge that morning. She had already ticked off zebra, buffalo, impala, wildebeest, warthog, baboon, common duiker and kudu. Out of the corner of her eye, she saw James also ticking off 'large-spotted genet' on his list.

'Hey! You can't tick off genet – you didn't see it!' Mandy protested, teasing her friend.

'Yes, I did – I just managed to get a glimpse of a twitching ear, I think,' said James, grinning at her.

Mandy laughed and Levina started up the Land-rover again. The noise of the engine startled a small herd of impala that had been grazing nearby. A beautiful reddish-brown buck sprinted away, leaping high as it went.

'Impala are wonderfully athletic, aren't they?' remarked Mandy's mum, Emily Hope.

Mandy watched the graceful animals disappearing into the bush and thought to herself how lucky she was to be here – on safari in the Ubungane Wildlife Reserve in South Africa, with James and her mum and dad. They had been in South Africa for just over a week now, visiting their friend, Dr Levina Lemiso. Mandy's parents, who were vets in the small Yorkshire village of Welford, had met Levina at veterinary college in York and been friends ever since. They had recently visited her when she was studying gorillas in the Congo. Now she was working at a research base in the Ubungane Wildlife Reserve.

Today, Levina was taking them on a tour of part of the reserve. 'Now here's an interesting creature,' she told them, slowing the Land-rover and pointing to the side of the road.

Eagerly, Mandy looked. A fat yellowish-grey snake with brown patches was zigzagging slowly over the low ridge of sand that edged the road.

'What kind of snake is that?' she asked, shuffling up to make room for James as he leaned over to look at the reptile.

'Puff adder,' Levina told them. 'Not a very pleasant customer – they're responsible for most of the snakebite deaths in South Africa.'

'Why's that?' asked James, curiously. 'There are loads of poisonous snakes, aren't there?'

'Well, it's sluggish and unlikely to get out of your way if you come upon one. But it can strike fast and does so without provocation,' explained Levina.

'I'm glad we're well out of its reach,' James said as he took a photograph of the snake.

Levina drove on. She steered round a bend and braked sharply as a giraffe suddenly stepped out from behind a tree a few metres further along the road. It took a couple of paces forward, then stopped and gazed down at them.

Mandy had never been so close to a giraffe before. She stared up at the huge animal towering above her. 'I feel like an insect!' she whispered to James who was slowly lifting his camera to take a picture.

'So do I,' he said, clicking the camera's shutter. 'I wonder how tall it is?'

'I'd say about five metres,' guessed Adam Hope. 'About as high as a two-storey building.'

The giraffe seemed quite unconcerned at being disturbed by the safari group. For several minutes it stood peacefully watching them. Then it casually loped across the road and into the bush. As it merged into the cover of the vegetation, Mandy became aware of a number of other giraffe deeper in the bush, camouflaged by the trees. There were at least half a dozen of them spaced quite far apart. Mandy suddenly noticed two faces peering down at them.

'Look, James,' she laughed, 'there are two heads sticking out of the top of that tree.'

'Like periscopes!' remarked James, gazing up at the enormous animals.

'They *do* look a bit like periscopes,' Mandy said. 'I suppose they must be able to see for miles.'

'Yes,' agreed James, 'and *they* don't need binoculars or glasses,' he added, cleaning some red dust off his specs.

'They *do* have excellent eyesight.' Levina agreed. 'They can see things that are almost invisible to us.'

'Really?' asked Mandy who was always keen to learn as much as she could about animals.

She wanted to be a vet one day, just like her parents.

'Yes.' Levina thought for a moment. 'Remember how hard it was to see that genet? Even after you noticed it and told us it was there, Mandy, it wasn't easy to spot it. It was really well camouflaged. Now, imagine a lion hiding in long grass. To the human eye, its colour is the same as the colour of the grass, which makes the lion almost invisible. A giraffe, on the other hand, can distinguish between the colour of the lion's coat and the colour of the grass, so it's able to make out the lion quite clearly.'

'That's a relief,' said Mandy, staring up at the heads that poked comically out from the tops of the trees. 'I'd hate to think they'd have no warning if a lion was about to pounce.'

'Lions have to pounce sometimes, though,' observed James, 'otherwise they'd starve.'

'That's right, Mandy – it's the law of the jungle!' remarked her dad. 'Or, in this case, the bush!'

'Mmm – I guess so,' agreed Mandy. 'But I'd rather the lions left giraffes off their menu.' She scanned the surrounding bush through her binoculars. 'I hope there aren't any lions lurking around here!'

'If there are, these giraffes stand a good chance of getting away,' Levina assured her, turning round in her seat. 'They can outrun a lion easily, and if they're trapped they can deliver a kick that can injure or kill an attacker.'

'That's good to know,' said Mandy focusing her binoculars on the giraffes once more.

'Sometimes, though, giraffes do end up on the menus of lions and other big predators,' continued Levina, 'especially when they're lying down or bending over with their front legs splayed while they drink. They're most vulnerable to attack then because it's very hard for them to get back up on their feet again quickly. That's why they hardly ever lie down to sleep and, when they do, it's only for about twenty minutes. When giraffes are sleeping, there's always at least one other giraffe standing by keeping watch.'

'Like a sentry?' suggested James.

'Absolutely!' Levina nodded. 'Another way they avoid danger is by not drinking very often. They manage to get most of the moisture they need from the leaves of the trees they eat.'

Mandy watched the giraffes stretching their long necks to browse on leaves in the upper reaches of the trees. Through her binoculars, she could see that the trees were covered in long spikes.

'Those trees are full of big thorns,' she commented. 'That must spoil the giraffes' meal a bit!'

'They look really sharp,' said James, 'Don't the giraffes' mouths and faces get scratched and cut?'

'Actually, they don't,' Levina assured them. 'Giraffes grasp the twigs and branches with their long tongues, which are very flexible and muscular, so they manage to avoid the thorns. Acacia trees are their favourite food.'

Mandy peered intently through her binoculars. 'Oh yes, I see what you mean. And look at their lips! They're almost rubbery – like something out of a cartoon,' she said, laughing.

As Mandy watched the giraffes chewing on the acacia branches, she noticed how the colour of their coats varied. She leaned forward to speak to Levina. 'Why do some of them have darker patches than others?' she asked.

'They're older than the others,' the scientist explained. 'As a giraffe ages, its coat darkens.'

'Aren't you doing research into giraffe markings, Levina?' asked Mrs Hope, who was sitting in the front passenger seat.

'Yes, I am,' said Levina, 'I'm interested in charting the patterns of giraffes' coats. Did you know that each giraffe has its own individual pattern – rather like human fingerprints?'

Mandy was intrigued. She looked more closely at the giraffes and tried to compare their markings.

James was also scrutinising the giraffes. 'I can't see any real differences,' he said at last, shaking his head and putting down his binoculars. 'I suppose you have to study them for hours before you really notice anything.'

'You *do* need to be patient,' Levina said, turning round and smiling at him. 'Shall we move on?' she asked.

Levina eased the Land-rover into gear and they moved off slowly in search of other wildlife. They drove along the dusty road that cut its way through the African savannah – home to scores of different species of animals. A leopard tortoise plodding across the road caused Levina to slow down. As Levina steered cautiously round the reptile, Emily Hope drew everyone's attention to a dung beetle she had spotted on the road a little way ahead of the vehicle.

'Please can we watch it for a bit?' asked Mandy,

standing up in her seat to look.

'Certainly,' said Levina, pulling up close to the beetle so that they could see it as it pushed and pulled a ball of dung at least twice its own size and weight towards the side of the road.

'Wow, that looks like hard work!' exclaimed James. 'Why does it do that?'

'The female lays her egg in the ball, then buries it,' explained Emily Hope. 'When the larva hatches, it feeds off the dung.'

James looked at Mandy and pulled a face.

'At last we've found something James doesn't want to eat!' Mandy grinned. She was absorbed, watching the activity of the little beetle. But her attention was interrupted by an urgent whisper from her father.

'Don't move,' he breathed, almost inaudibly. 'There's a pride of lions in a clearing just beyond the tall grass over there!'

Hardly daring to breathe, Mandy stared into the bush. The lions' coats merged perfectly with the colour of the grass as Levina had said, but she was able to spot four cubs gambolling about, their playfulness giving the pride away.

'Well, that's lucky,' murmured Levina, 'Some people never get to see any lions during their stay.

And a whole pride, complete with cubs, is a real bonus.'

Mandy was enthralled. The cubs chased, pounced, tumbled, leaped and somersaulted. They batted each other with their large fluffy paws and climbed intrepidly over the adults, which yawned and stretched, displaying their sharp teeth and claws, then lazily heaved their powerful bodies upright and started to move off.

'I expect they're going hunting,' said James with an edge of excitement to his voice.

'Well, if they are, I'm glad they're moving in the opposite direction from the giraffes,' Mandy commented.

Great swathes of pink and blue decorated the western sky as the sun gradually sank lower, slipping suddenly below the horizon. Mandy was always surprised at how quickly the darkness came in Africa.

'Well, seeing as the lions have set off to get their dinner, I think we ought to be doing the same,' suggested Levina as she started up the Land-rover.

'Can't we wait a bit longer to see some of the nocturnal animals coming out?' pleaded Mandy.

'Not today,' said her mother. 'If we wait any longer we'll miss dinner and I don't think Dad and James would be very happy about that.' She looked at her husband who was sitting in the back and smiled. 'Perhaps we can book to go on a night drive later in the week.'

'Oh, yes please!' cried Mandy. 'That'll be great, won't it, James?'

James nodded enthusiastically.

'And, if you like,' said Levina, 'you can join me and Sipho tomorrow. We're leaving at dawn to go down to the southern part of the reserve, which is closed to visitors, to observe the giraffe population there.'

Sipho Ngomane was the manager of the research station where Levina worked. The previous week he had shown Mandy and James how leopards were tracked from the base.

'I'd love to go,' said Mandy, 'wouldn't you, James?' Again, James nodded enthusiastically. 'Please may we go?' Mandy asked her parents

'Well,' said Mr Hope looking at his wife, 'I don't know about you, Emily, but I think I'd rather spend the day relaxing back at the Lodge. After all we *are* on holiday and I think we get enough opportunities to get up at the crack of dawn back at home during the lambing season!'

'Me too, Adam,' replied Emily Hope. 'But if

Levina doesn't mind Mandy and James joining her, then I don't mind either – just as long as you two don't get in the way.'

'We won't get in the way, will we, James?' Mandy promised at once.

'Absolutely not!' said James solemnly.

Dinner that night was a *braai* – an African barbecue. It took place in an outdoor area called a *lapa* where all the guests staying at the Lodge had gathered. Even though it was already autumn in South Africa, the evening was balmy. Levina was sitting at a table when the Hope family and James arrived. They made their way over to her, past the *braai* on which a variety of meats and vegetables were sizzling. The aroma of the cooking food made Mandy's mouth water. She hadn't realised how hungry she was.

As she sat down, Mandy saw David, the thirteen-year-old son of Pam and Tony Mackenzie, the owners of Ubungane Lodge. Mandy waved to him and he came over to greet them.

'Would you like to eat with us, David, or are you waiting for your parents?' Emily Hope asked him.

'Oh, yes please,' he replied. 'Mum and Dad and

Sophie won't be here for a while.' Sophie was David's nine-year-old sister.

'Pull up a chair then,' said Mr Hope.

David took a chair from the next table and put it down next to Mandy. 'Have you had a good day?' he asked.

'Very good,' she said, shuffling her chair along to make room for him. 'We've been out on safari with Levina.'

'We saw a pride of lions with their cubs,' James told him.

David looked surprised. 'You're lucky,' he said. 'We hardly ever see lions. You've only been here a week and already you've seen a whole pride!'

Just then a gong sounded. Kitunga, the chef, announced that the food was ready and guests began to queue up to help themselves. As she waited in the queue with James and David, Mandy looked up at the night sky.

'Isn't that the Southern Cross?' she asked, pointing towards a constellation of stars

'Yes, that's right,' David replied. 'And, look, there's a meteorite.'

Mandy watched the bright spot of light plunging towards the horizon. 'A shooting star! Quick, let's make a wish!' she laughed. 'I wish the giraffes we saw earlier will be safe from the lions!'

'In that case, I wish the lions have a good night's hunting,' James retorted, smiling.

They made their way along the buffet, filling their plates with delicious food. Mandy chose vegetable kebabs and peppers stuffed with rice. She made her way back to their table, followed by David and James.

'Just as well we got there before you three,' laughed Adam Hope, staring at the mound of food on James's plate. 'Otherwise there wouldn't have been anything left for us.'

As the guests settled down to eat, a quiet hum replaced the earlier hubbub of conversation. Mandy could hear the sounds of nocturnal creatures from the darkness beyond – singing crickets, croaking frogs, the shriek of a nightjar and a loud 'whoo-hooop' sound that she didn't recognise.

'What was that?' she asked, turning to Levina.

'Spotted hyena,' said Levina. 'You've heard of the laughing hyena, haven't you?'

Mandy nodded.

'Well, that was its call,' Levina told her. 'It's an odd noise, isn't it?'

The hyena's laugh subsided and gave way to a

distinctive, low 'uumh-hummph' rumbling sound, which gradually tailed off leaving an almost eerie silence in the air.

'And what was that?' asked James.

'That,' said Levina, with a grin, 'was the roar of a lion.'

# Two

Mandy was woken early the next morning by the high-pitched whine of a mosquito. She pulled the pillow over her head to block out the monotonous noise so she could go back to sleep. The *braai* had gone on late into the night and she was exhausted. But then she suddenly remembered Levina's last words to her as they had all headed for bed. 'We'll meet you in the carpark at six o'clock tomorrow morning – don't be late!'

Mandy sat up with a start. She'd nearly forgotten they were going out into the reserve with Levina and Sipho today. What was the time? It was still dark so it couldn't be too late, surely? She switched on her bedside lamp and reached for her watch. It was quarter past five, plenty of time to get dressed and have breakfast. But first, Mandy decided that she'd better check that James was awake.

'James,' she called softly.

There was no reply. Mandy walked round the screen that divided their room to find that James was sleeping soundly. She shook his shoulder gently but without success, so she shook him more vigorously. He grumbled crossly, turned over and went on sleeping.

Mandy switched on the light. 'Wake up – or I'll pour this jug of water over you!' she threatened, reaching for the jug on the bedside table. James just groaned again.

'Come on, wake up!' Mandy insisted. 'We're supposed to be ready at six o'clock. Otherwise Levina will go without us. Have you forgotten we're going out to see the giraffes with her and Sipho today?'

At last, James sat up in bed, rubbing his eyes. He fumbled for his glasses on the bedside table. 'What's the time?' he muttered.

'Quarter past five,' Mandy told him cheerfully.

'Quarter past five! You must be mad. It's

much too early,' moaned James. He took off his glasses, lay down again and switched off the light.

Switching the light back on, Mandy handed him his glasses. 'Don't go back to sleep now, otherwise you won't wake up in time,' she told him. 'You don't want to miss breakfast, do you?'

Leaving James to get up, Mandy grabbed her towel, a clean T-shirt and pair of shorts and made her way to the reed-enclosed outdoor shower-room adjoining Leela's Lodge, the cabin in which they were staying. The guest rooms at the Lodge were separate cabins, named after animals found in the reserve. Their cabin was named after an orphaned leopard cub, Leela, who had been raised on the reserve. Leela was now an adult and had been successfully released into the wild by Sandie Howard, a big-cats expert who had worked at the base. Mandy and James had helped Sandie when Leela's cubs had gone missing the week before.

Mandy showered and dressed then went back inside to brush her hair. She looked around for a scrunchie to tie her hair up in a ponytail. She thought she'd left a red one on the dressing-table yesterday, but there was no sign of it. She didn't want to waste time looking for things, so she took out a new one.

She could hear James moving about, getting dressed on his side of the screen. A few minutes later, he came into the little sitting area where she was waiting for him and looked around with a puzzled expression on his face.

'Lost something?' Mandy asked.

'I don't know,' he replied. 'I bought a packet of cashew nuts yesterday to take with us today in the Land-rover, but I can't find them now. Oh well, I must have put them somewhere else. Let's go and get some breakfast.' He hoisted his camera and binoculars over his shoulder and headed for the door.

They made their way along the path towards the dining-room in the main building of Ubungane Lodge. The sky was growing lighter in the east and the birds were just beginning to stir, making odd little chirping and twittering noises. Beyond the game-proof fence surrounding the Lodge grounds, Mandy could make out the shapes of buck and zebra grazing peacefully.

Then, from a large tree in the garden nearby, a loud chattering noise broke the early morning calm. The branches of the tree swayed and bounced as if in the grip of a violent storm, but all around the air was still. The chattering continued and Mandy and James went closer to the tree to investigate. As they drew nearer, the chattering intensified and so did the swaying of the branches. All of a sudden, out of the tree, several small animals seemed to be hurled into the air and propelled into another tree about five metres away.

'Vervet monkeys!' Mandy laughed, watching in amusement as the little primates launched themselves haphazardly into space and then, with an almost casual reach of their long grey arms, grabbed the branches of the neighbouring tree.

In the dining-room, cereal and fruit had been left out for Mandy and James by the staff the night before. They had just finished eating when Lindiwe Ngomane, the daughter of the manager of the research centre, arrived. Lindiwe was thirteen, a year older than Mandy.

'Hi,' she said, 'I'm coming with you today. My father and Levina asked me to fetch you. They want to get going as soon as they can.'

Mandy and James picked up their baseball caps and binoculars and followed Lindiwe outside. Near the entrance to the dining-room, Mandy noticed a cornflakes box lying at the base of a tree. She was surprised to see litter lying about. 'That's odd,' she said, puzzled. 'The grounds are normally so tidy.'

'I don't think my mother will be too pleased to see that,' said Lindiwe, whose mother, Mmatsatsi, worked in the office at the Lodge.

But there was no time to stop and clear up – Levina and Sipho were waiting. They reached the carpark just as the sun was beginning to rise like a glowing orange ball in the eastern sky.

'Hi, Levina, hi, Sipho,' said Mandy as they clambered into the Land-rover.

'*Sakubona*,' said Sipho, raising a hand in greeting.

'Morning, you two,' Levina replied. 'I was wondering if you'd make it after such a late night – I had a hard time getting up myself!'

'So did James!' laughed Mandy, poking her friend in the ribs.

'No, I didn't,' protested James, grinning broadly and settling into his seat.

Mandy felt a sense of anticipation as they set off. She felt honoured to be allowed to visit a section of the reserve that was out of bounds to most people. She turned to Lindiwe who was sitting next to her. 'It must be great living here and being able to see wildlife every day,' she remarked.

'Yes, I love living at Ubungane,' said Lindiwe, smiling. 'But I don't often go into the reserve any more because I'm at school most of the time.'

'Is your school near here?' asked James, adjusting his baseball cap.

'No, there's no school in the bush,' Lindiwe told him. 'My school is at Babanango. It takes three hours to drive there, so I have to stay there in term time. I only come home for the holidays.'

Mandy turned her attention once more to the countryside around them. Now and then she caught sight of animals she would have liked to watch for a while, but knowing that Levina and Sipho were eager to get on with their work, she didn't ask them to stop. However, when she caught a glimpse of something moving in the undergrowth close to the side of the road, she couldn't help crying out, 'Oh, please stop, Levina, – I think I saw something interesting.'

'All right – just this once,' Levina replied, and she reversed the Land-rover a short way and turned off the engine.

There was barely a movement in the bush.

Mandy stared at the spot where she thought she'd seen something. 'I must have been mistaken,' she said. 'Sorry, Levina.'

Levina was leaning forward to turn the keys in the ignition again when suddenly Sipho put up his hand to silence them all.

'Leopard,' he whispered. Less than five metres from them, a leopard was stealthily weaving its way through dense thickets, a large bird dangling from its jaws. Mandy watched in awe.

'Guinea fowl for breakfast,' remarked Levina. 'It's getting late for a leopard – she'll be off to sleep in the shade soon.'

Then, just as suddenly as it had appeared, the leopard had gone.

For the next hour, they drove southwards, stopping occasionally to let herds of buck or groups of warthogs cross the road in front of them. The day was growing steadily warmer.

'Let's stop for a cool drink,' suggested Sipho.

'Good idea, *Baba*,' said Lindiwe. 'I'm parched!'

'OK, I'll pull in at the Ulwandele waterhole ahead so we can sit in the shade of the fever trees there,' said Levina.

'Maybe we'll see some animals in need of a

drink too,' said James, fanning himself with his baseball cap.

'More than likely,' Levina replied, steering off the road and on to a rough narrow track. The Land-rover rattled and dipped as Levina negotiated the bumpy track. Eventually, they reached a wide flat area surrounding a big pool of muddy water, fringed by tall fever trees. On the far side of the waterhole, Mandy could see a small group of giraffes stripping the leaves and young shoots from the tops of some of the trees. To the right of them, three more giraffes were bending down at the pool, drinking the muddy water. Their front legs were splayed in front of them as their long necks reached down.

'Don't they look uncomfortable!' Mandy exclaimed.

'Mmmm, they do look awkward in that position but that's the only way they can reach the water,' Levina said. She parked the Land-rover beneath a fever tree that stood a little way back from the waterhole. 'Despite having such long necks, it's not enough for them to simply bend down – they have to splay their legs like that to get down to the level of the water,' she explained.

'You should be able to get some good photos of

these giraffes,' Mandy said to James, who was already fiddling with his camera lens.

'They look great, don't they?' he replied. 'This is the first chance I've had to get pictures of giraffes drinking.'

'Can we get out to stretch our legs, *Baba*?' Lindiwe asked, leaning over the front seat to speak to her father.

'OK, but you must all stay close,' Sipho cautioned them. 'You never know what's hiding in the bush. James, can you reach the cool box? It's just behind you.'

They climbed out of the Land-rover, trying to make as little noise as possible so as not to frighten the giraffes. Mandy stretched, relieved to be able to get out of the vehicle, but she knew that the rifle Sipho had slung over his shoulders was what made it possible for them to stand in the open. She had seen signs all over the reserve warning visitors not to get out of their cars except at specially designated rest areas.

'Help yourselves to a drink,' said Levina, opening the cool box and taking out a small bottle of fruit juice for herself.

Mandy chose a guava juice and sipped it as she watched the giraffes drinking. After a while, two

of the giraffes at the waterhole slowly heaved themselves back into an upright position and joined the others, browsing amongst the trees.

'I see what you mean about how hard it is for a giraffe to stand up,' Mandy told Levina. 'It looked like a huge effort for those two. Did you get a shot of them, James?' she asked.

James had replaced the lens cap on his camera and was now digging in the cool box for a drink.

'Yes, I'm hoping it'll come out OK,' he said. 'But I'll take another picture when that one gets up.' He pointed to the remaining giraffe at the waterhole.

Mandy noticed that it had stopped drinking. It had raised its neck and was trying to get up. It swung its neck to one side but without success. It remained stuck, with its legs splayed apart.

'That one seems to be having a lot more trouble than the other two,' said Mandy as the giraffe continued to struggle. 'Do you think it's OK, Levina?'

Levina shook her head, 'I'm not sure,' she replied. 'It certainly seems to be having more difficulty than usual. Perhaps its front feet are stuck in the mud.'

Mandy looked through her binoculars. Levina was right. The giraffe's front hooves were completely submerged in the thick mud and the more it tried to get free, the deeper its feet sank. It began to swing its mighty neck from side to side.

'It's trying to get some leverage to stand up,' Sipho told them.

'How will that work?' asked James, edging his way forward as he watched the giraffe.

'Sometimes, a very powerful upward swing of the neck gives a giraffe enough thrust to pull itself upright,' explained Sipho.

'Yes, I saw one do that once,' said Lindiwe. 'It

was also standing in thick mud.'

'I hope it works this time,' said Mandy anxiously. 'It really does look very vulnerable.' She was all too well aware that predators could soon start gathering to finish the giraffe off. 'The poor animal,' she sighed. 'It won't stand much chance if there are lions about.'

'I know it's hard, Mandy,' sympathised Levina, 'but it's nature. It may seem cruel to us, but lions have to eat too and, being carnivores, they need to eat other animals. It's all about survival of the fittest – and right now that giraffe is not the fittest.'

Mandy nodded miserably. 'I know,' she said. 'But it just seems so unfair because the giraffe can't do anything to protect itself.'

'These are wild animals, not pets, Mandy,' Lindiwe reminded her.

'That's true,' said Sipho. 'Out here in the wild, everything is just a link in the food chain. You have to leave your heart behind when you go into the wilderness. Now, I think it is time to move on.'

They clambered back into the Land-rover, and Levina started the engine. As they drove away, abandoning the giraffe to its fate, Mandy knew

she could never leave her heart behind when she
visited the bush.

# Three

They drove along the dusty roads traversing the savannah for about half an hour. Zebra, wildebeest, buffalo and various species of buck dotted the landscape. Mandy spotted powerful raptors high in the cloudless sky, soaring ever upwards on thermal draughts, their sharp eyes keenly seeking prey on the earth far below.

Occasionally Levina and Sipho pointed out less common animals, such as a pair of honey-badgers that were scraping and scratching at a fallen tree trunk.

'Their other name is ratel because of the rattling sound they make,' Sipho told them quietly, as they watched from the Land-rover.

'Why are they scraping at that tree trunk?' asked James, after he'd taken a photo.

'I think they've found a bees' nest,' Levina explained. 'They open up the nest so they can eat the young bees and the honey, which are their favourite foods.'

Mandy winced at the thought of eating bees – it didn't sound very appetising to her.

A small grey bird flitted from branch to branch in a tree overhanging the scene. 'Ah yes, there's sure to be some honey there,' Sipho said. 'That bird is a honeyguide. It knows where there's honey about and it will wait for the badgers to expose the nest, to get its share.'

Mandy loved watching all the different wildlife in the bush, but she couldn't stop thinking about the distressed giraffe. They passed a flock of whitebacked vultures squabbling aggressively over the carcass of an ill-fated antelope. 'I suppose the giraffe at the waterhole could be next,' she said, shuddering at the thought.

'Probably,' agreed Levina. 'But you can see that nothing out here is waste.'

Levina and Sipho were constantly on the lookout for signs of giraffe. Every now and then,

Sipho would jump out to inspect droppings and spoor. At last he found fresh dung, indicating that a large herd had passed that way not long before.

'But there are also tracks of other animals,' he told them as he climbed back into the Land-rover. 'It looks as though a pair of lions is following the giraffes.' Mandy shuddered at the thought.

The tracks crossed the road and then faded into the bush. Sipho was certain that the giraffes – and the lions – had been heading in the direction of the waterhole.

'I'm hoping it's the herd I've been monitoring,' said Levina. 'The last time I saw them, they weren't far from here. Once we catch up with them, I'll be able to tell by looking at their markings.'

Levina turned the Land-rover and they retraced their journey, all the while looking for signs of the giraffes. They neared the track leading to the Ulwandele waterhole and Levina suggested that the herd might have congregated there. 'We'll have a look,' she said, steering off the road. As they bounced along the rutted track, Mandy desperately hoped that the lions had taken a different route. Anxiously, she peered ahead, hoping that the giraffe had managed to free itself from its muddy prison.

The waterhole came into view. Levina's herd was nowhere to be seen but there, still stuck firmly in the mud, was the lone giraffe. Its attempts to free itself were now much weaker than before. Its head and neck drooped feebly and its front legs quivered from the strain of having been stretched for so long. The animal was obviously exhausted and in a state of despair. Its previously serene facial expression had been replaced by a look of sheer misery.

Mandy noticed that the rest of the small herd that had been browsing in the area was beginning to move off. 'They're not even looking back,' she cried, feeling close to tears. 'It's as if they've given up on it! Now it has no defence at all. Oh, I hope those lions aren't anywhere near here!'

'If they *are* nearby, it won't take them long to find the giraffe,' said Levina.

'Will they smell it?' asked James.

'No, they don't seem to use scent to detect live prey,' Levina answered. 'But they drink regularly so it's only a matter of time before they get here.'

'It'll be a surprise for them to come across food they don't have to hunt!' observed James, looking at the giraffe thoughtfully.

Mandy frowned. 'Don't you think that's a bit unfair?' she asked, feeling irritated with her friend.

'Not really,' he replied quietly.

'But it *is* unfair,' insisted Mandy, turning away from him in annoyance. 'The giraffe doesn't stand a chance against lions, stuck like this.'

'I know that, but remember what Levina said about the survival of the fittest,' James replied.

'But the giraffe *is* fit,' protested Mandy. 'Or it was, until it got stuck. There's nothing actually *wrong* with it,' she said, watching the giraffe raise its neck in an almost half-hearted attempt to pull itself up. 'It just needs to be able to get free.'

James was silent. Mandy wondered what he was thinking. He took off his glasses and wiped them with his T-shirt, then looked at Mandy and said, 'But if it can't get free, then it can't run off and so it *isn't* fit any more. It becomes prey for the predators.'

'But don't you feel sorry for the giraffe?' Mandy protested. James usually cared so much about animals. She couldn't understand how he could be so casual about leaving the giraffe to die.

'A bit, I suppose,' he said, putting his glasses back on. 'But what about the lions?'

'What do you mean?' asked Mandy.

'They have to survive too. They have to get food for themselves and their cubs. So they have to kill something,' he pointed out. 'And why not *this* giraffe?'

'Because it doesn't stand a chance of getting away,' Mandy insisted, annoyed that he didn't seem to understand. She leaned forward to speak to Levina and Sipho. 'Isn't there something we can do to help it?' she begged.

'I'm sorry, Mandy,' Sipho said softly. 'There's nothing we can do.'

'But there must be!' she cried. 'Can't we wait for a while and then, if the lions do come, you could fire your rifle to scare them off?' she asked Sipho. 'At least then the giraffe would have more time to try to get out of the mud.'

'I don't think so,' said Levina, leaning back in her seat and running her hands through her hair. 'There's no point in trying to buy time for the giraffe – it's not going to be able to free itself. If we try to scare the lions off, sooner or later they'll return. We would just be prolonging the giraffe's suffering. I agree with Sipho, Mandy, nothing can be done.'

Mandy thought of the times she had helped to

rescue other animals in distress. There *had* to be a way of helping this giraffe. Surely there must be some way to get it out of the mud.

Sipho turned around in his seat. 'I can see that you're hurting for the giraffe, *nkosazana*,' he said gently. 'I understand that hurt. When I was about the same age as you, I watched a proud young zebra fighting for its life in the jaws of a crocodile. For many months afterwards, I could still hear the cry of that zebra as it fought bravely to free itself. But the crocodile won and dragged it to its death under the water.'

Mandy pictured the event. 'It must have been terrible,' she said.

'Yes,' agreed Lindiwe quietly. 'I don't think I'd like to see something like that.'

'It *was* terrible,' said Sipho. 'But things like that happen all the time. Life in the bush can be very harsh,' he continued. 'But you must try to understand that we cannot involve ourselves in these situations.'

'Do you mean because it's too dangerous?' asked James, who had been leaning forward to listen.

'Yes, that's one reason, but mainly because the policy of the Ubungane Research Centre is the same policy of most people working in nature conservation,' Sipho explained. 'We do not interfere in nature; we have to let it run its course. Otherwise, if we place human values on things that happen in the wild, we may be in danger of upsetting the natural balance.'

'But surely we won't be upsetting the balance if we save just one giraffe?' Mandy said, fighting back her tears.

'If we save this giraffe, then we have to save all the others that are in danger from attack,' Sipho said. 'And then how will the lions survive, and the crocodiles? What will become of the predators? How will we prevent the giraffes and buck and zebras from multiplying so much that one day there is not enough space for them and not enough food for them to eat? Can you see how important this natural balance is – important not only for the animals, but for us humans too?'

Mandy couldn't answer. She knew that what Sipho was saying made sense, but she hated to think of the giraffe being left to its fate.

Sipho continued. 'Remember what Levina was saying earlier about the food chain?'

Mandy nodded.

'Well, think of this chain as a flowing river,' he said. 'The river is created by lots of small tributaries that form when it rains. The river gets bigger as each tributary joins into it. Eventually, the river flows into the mighty sea. Every drop of water that went into that river has now become a part of the sea.' Sipho shifted in his seat then went on with his explanation. 'And so it is with everything in the wild,' he said, gesturing broadly towards the waterhole and the surrounding bush. 'It starts at the bottom, with the insects, the grass and other plants, which feed animals like the giraffes, and at the top of the chain are the predators like the mighty lion. Every part of the chain one day becomes part of the lion.'

'I suppose you could say that the lion owns the giraffe,' commented Lindiwe.

'That is one way of looking at it,' said her father gently.

'And if we interfere, we'll break the chain.' James was fiddling with his baseball cap.

Mandy looked unhappily at James. Then she leaned back in her seat and sighed. 'I can't bear to think of this giraffe being eaten alive by the lions.' She raised her binoculars and focused on the giraffe's face. Its large almond-shaped eyes were partially closed. Mandy could see that it had given up its fight. 'You poor thing,' she murmured quietly.

'You must try not to think about it, Mandy,' said Sipho. 'We should leave now. But listen, death will come quickly to the giraffe because lions are skilled killers and will suffocate it immediately. They will not eat it alive. The giraffe may know fear for a very small moment and then it will know nothing. That, I can promise you. Let's go, Levina.' Sipho turned in his seat to face the front again.

'OK,' said Levina, preparing to turn the Land-rover.

Mandy took one last look back at the giraffe. As she did so, she became aware of something emerging from behind a fever tree, not far from the giraffe. A giraffe calf stepped cautiously out into the open.

'Oh, Levina, stop, *please*,' she cried. 'You *must* stop! There's a baby giraffe – it's been left behind,' cried Mandy.

Levina braked and they all turned to watch as the calf picked its way warily across to the adult.

'That must be its mother,' Lindiwe said.

'Mmmm, I think you're right,' agreed Levina, studying the calf through her binoculars. 'It's a very young male – probably no more than about three weeks old – so it will still be very dependent on its mother. That's why it didn't leave with the rest of the herd.'

The calf stopped at the right flank of the adult giraffe. It looked anxious and, without the full protection of its mother, very vulnerable. It was clear to Mandy that even though the calf was more than two metres tall, it could never defend itself against a lion.

'I suppose it'll just stay here and the lions will kill it too,' Mandy said sadly.

'Yes – that's most probably what will happen,' Sipho agreed. 'Without his mother to look after him, he is as vulnerable as she is. If she was standing upright and the lions attacked, she'd have a good chance of driving them off.'

'Couldn't the calf just run off?' asked James. 'That would be better than just waiting to be killed.'

'Well, it *could*,' Levina said. 'A young calf can run almost as swiftly as an adult – about forty-five kilometres an hour – but I doubt very much that it will run off, as it doesn't have its mother to lead the way.'

'It wouldn't be able to survive without its

mother anyway,' said Mandy. 'Oh, I wish it had a chance.'

The calf nestled against the adult giraffe, trying to shelter underneath her. But with her forelegs splayed the mother was too low, and the calf had to stand to one side of her instead. He flicked his tail, snorted softly and then began to nudge his mother – almost as if he were trying to help her get up, Mandy thought. But all his mother could do was turn her neck back to lick and nuzzle her baby.

Mandy desperately wished she could do

something to save the pair. She willed the calf to run off, to find the herd and safety amongst others. But he remained snuggled against his mother. Like hers, his fate was sealed.

Mandy wondered just how long it would be before lions appeared. Perhaps they were already close by, keeping their distance from a vehicle full of humans. Perhaps they were just waiting for the Land-rover to leave, before they pounced and made their kill.

# Four

Mandy expected Levina to start the engine and drive off. But, instead, she sat watching the giraffes and appeared to be in deep thought. After a few moments, she turned to Sipho and said, 'It strikes me that we could be missing a good research opportunity if we *do* just drive away.'

'What do you mean?' asked Mandy eagerly, thinking perhaps there was hope after all.

Levina looked back at Mandy. 'Well, I'm not just looking at the markings of individual giraffes – I'm also interested in studying the communication and bonding between members of a herd,' she explained. She glanced at the two giraffes. 'Watching this pair in this tricky situation makes me think that if I could observe them for a while at close quarters, I could learn quite a lot about the way they relate to one another.'

'Do you think you might see behaviour nobody has seen before?' James sounded interested.

'It is possible,' said Levina. 'I'd like to see if they display any special behaviour following this kind of traumatic incident.'

'So you want us to intervene?' asked Sipho guardedly.

'I think it's worth considering, Sipho,' Levina sounded quite enthusiastic now. 'If we could rescue them – and as long as the mother isn't seriously injured – we could take them back to the research base and house them in a *boma* for a while until the mother is ready to be returned to the bush. Then I'd be able to observe their habits and behaviour at close quarters.'

'And we could watch them too!' said Lindiwe, smiling at Mandy and James.

Mandy felt a wave of excitement rising in her. She pictured the *boma*. It was a large enclosure that was used for animals that were brought to the research centre, a substantial area of the bush with a high wooden fence around it. The conditions in the *boma* were as close as possible to the natural surroundings, so the giraffes would be quite at home. Mandy held her breath, hoping that Sipho would agree to Levina's suggestion.

Sipho was silent, his chin resting in his right hand. He lifted his binoculars and studied the giraffes for a few moments. Then, at last, he spoke. 'I suppose it *would* be possible to get the giraffe out of the mud,' he said slowly. 'But that's not our only problem here. We must think very carefully about what we would be doing.' He looked at Mandy, James and Lindiwe in the back seat. 'What is happening here is very natural in the wild,' he told them seriously, 'especially when a species is as plentiful as the giraffes are at Ubungane. If we come between the giraffes and their natural predators we would be creating an abnormal environment.'

'We'd be breaking the chain,' suggested James.

Sipho nodded. Mandy felt her hopes being dashed, and felt angry with James for not supporting Levina's idea and jeopardising their chance to save the giraffe. She was about to argue, when Levina spoke.

'I know you're right, Sipho, but I can't help feeling that this is a wonderful opportunity for research,' she said. 'I think it would be worthwhile.'

'Mmm,' Sipho was frowning. 'I have to consider the cost, though,' he said.

'What cost?' asked Mandy anxiously.

'Getting the mother out of the mud and into the game truck wouldn't be an easy operation,' Sipho told her. 'There are always dangers – not only to the giraffe but to the rescuers as well.'

Mandy's hopes sank further. She knew Sipho was right – capturing wild animals was a dangerous business. A kick from a giraffe could kill a lion and there was always the possibility that it would kick out at the rescuers. And Mandy knew enough about wild animals to realise that the stress of the rescue could harm the giraffe too. But even so . . .

When Levina spoke, it was almost as if she had read Mandy's thoughts. 'I suppose the biggest danger is of someone getting kicked by the giraffe.' She turned to the three in the back. 'The problem is that it could be dangerous to sedate the giraffe.'

Mandy was puzzled. 'Can't you use a tranquilliser dart?' she asked.

'I wish we could, but it would be too risky,' answered Levina.

'Why's that?' asked James, sounding curious.

'Giraffes are very sensitive animals and can react badly to tranquillisers, as well as to the antidote used to bring them out of their sedated state. There would be no point in sedating the giraffe just to have her die because of it,' explained Levina.

'And that's not all,' added Sipho, climbing out of the Land-rover and slinging his rifle over his shoulder. 'Sedatives cost money,' he told them, 'and we don't have the funds at the research centre to use that kind of drug often. We have to restrict ourselves to using them in vital situations only – like the black rhino relocation exercise we carried out a few weeks ago.'

'Why was that vital?' asked James, stretching his arms above his head.

'Well, black rhinos are endangered. So we do all we can to try to preserve the species and increase their numbers. We relocated a male rhino to another game park which has very few males,' said Sipho.

'The research centre was helping the whole species,' added Lindiwe. 'With animals that are plentiful, like the giraffes, there is no real need to help them.' She stood up and stretched too.

'*Baba*,' she said, turning to her father, 'can we get out? I'm stiff.'

'Yes,' answered Sipho. 'But I'm going over there to take a closer look – you stay by the Land-rover.'

'Are you going to see if the giraffe *can* be pulled out of the mud? Mandy asked, as she opened the door and clambered out.

'I want to assess the situation,' he answered. 'If we try to rescue this giraffe, it has to cost as little as possible and that means it needs to be quite a straightforward operation with the minimum of danger.' Sipho turned and strode off towards the waterhole.

Mandy looked at Lindiwe and James anxiously. 'I hope he decides it looks easy enough,' she said.

Levina touched her gently on the shoulder. 'Sipho is very cautious. He'll need to be thoroughly persuaded that a rescue would be fairly uncomplicated and worthwhile. Try not to expect too much,' she warned.

Mandy watched as Sipho reached the waterhole. He stopped and stood opposite the giraffe, which was about ten metres away from him on the other side of the waterhole. He crouched down and felt the mud, then stood again and pushed at the mud with his strong boots.

Mandy could almost heart her heart thumping as she waited to see how the giraffes would react to him. The calf hadn't moved from its mother's side. It stared at Sipho, then glanced around nervously, as if it was aware of some danger in the bush that Mandy couldn't see. From time to time, the adult giraffe reached back with her neck to nuzzle the baby, but it seemed to cost her a lot of effort. She looked very tired.

'The mother must be so frightened,' murmured Mandy. 'I wonder if she's injured as well as stuck?'

'That would be a problem,' said Levina. 'If she *is* badly hurt, then we'd probably have to destroy her and the calf.'

Mandy bit her lip. 'Is that because it would cost too much to treat her?' she asked sadly.

'Yes, drugs are expensive and I'm afraid I can't spend so much of my time looking after just two animals,' Levina told her. 'And there's also the question of keeping the pair at the *boma* for an extended period while the mother is recovering. They would become too domesticated and that would put them in danger when they were released back into the bush.'

'Is that because they'd have lost their fear of man?' asked James.

'Not just their fear of man,' Levina replied. 'After a long stay in a sheltered environment, they would have become less sensitive to signs of other kinds of danger. They would almost certainly fall prey to big cats before they could get used to being in the wild again.'

Lindiwe had been listening thoughtfully to the discussion. 'Then we would be the ones to cause the giraffes to die,' she commented.

'That's true,' remarked Levina. 'Of course, there's also the possibility that the giraffe will be in good shape, and then we'd have to let her go,' she added. 'I couldn't justify taking them back to the *boma*, if they don't need *any* time to recover. Anyway, let's not speculate – let's wait for Sipho's decision.'

Mandy realised that Levina was right. There would be no point in going to all the trouble and expense of rescuing the giraffes and treating any serious injuries if, at the end of it all, they'd be no better off then they were at that moment. And if the giraffe *wasn't* hurt, it would be pointless taking her and the calf back to the *boma*. It all seemed so complicated.

Sipho had finished inspecting the waterhole and was walking back towards the Land-rover.

'He looks cheerful,' Mandy whispered. 'Perhaps he's going to say yes.'

'Let's hope you're right,' smiled Levina. 'So, what do you say, Sipho?' she asked, as the base manager approached. 'Do we try to mount a rescue for the sake of a research opportunity or do we just leave nature to take its course?'

Sipho took off his hat and wiped his brow with his sleeve. 'Well, I've had a good look at the conditions there and I think it could be possible to get a vehicle close enough to pull the giraffe out.' Mandy felt her heart miss a beat. Sipho continued, 'So – I think that Levina the scientist wins! We'll try to make use of this situation for research.'

'Oh, thank you!' exclaimed Mandy with relief.

'Wait a minute, *nkosazana*,' Sipho cautioned her. 'First I need to check with Anton, our game capture specialist. If he thinks that rescuing this giraffe for research would not be worth the risk to our team, then we will have to give up on the idea. I'll radio back to the base and find out what he thinks.'

Sipho reached into the Land-rover for the radio. Mandy was on tenterhooks as he contacted the base. Anton just *had* to say that they could manage the rescue.

'Come in base, come in. Over,' called Sipho.

'Base here,' came a crackled reply. 'What can I do for you, Sipho? Over.'

'Is Anton there? Over,' Sipho asked.

'He was here a few minutes ago. I'll see if he's still around. Over,' said the voice from the base.

'Ok, I'll wait to hear from you. Over and out,' replied Sipho. He pulled himself up on to the bull-bars at the front of the Land-rover and sat there with the radio in his lap. 'Let's hope he hasn't gone too far,' he said.

Levina sat down at the base of a fever tree a

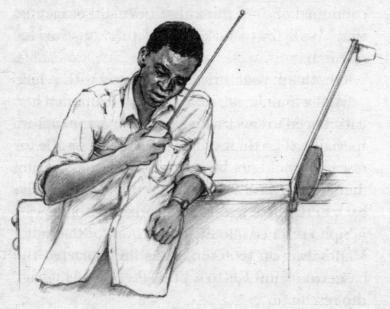

few metres away and leaned against the sulphur-green trunk. She pulled her cap down over her eyes and said, 'Might as well get some rest while we wait.'

Lindiwe and James also rested against the tree trunk but Mandy pulled herself up next to Sipho on the Land-rover. She wanted to make sure she didn't miss a word of what Anton said when he answered.

A few minutes later, Sipho's radio crackled into life again.

'Come in, Sipho, come in. Anton here. Over,' called Anton in the strong South African accent that Mandy was at last beginning to get used to.

'Ah, Anton. We're at the Ulwandele waterhole. An adult female giraffe has been stuck in the mud for some time,' explained Sipho. 'She has a young calf and Levina thinks she'd like to study them back at the base. Any chance of rescuing them? Over.'

Hearing the conversation, James and Lindiwe jumped up from their resting spot and hurried across to the Land-rover.

'Rescue giraffes?' Anton sounded puzzled.

'Levina thinks it will be useful to her. Over,' replied Sipho.

'Can you give me some more details? Over,' came Anton's response.

Mandy listened intently as Sipho explained the situation more fully to Anton. 'I don't think the mud is too bad,' Sipho was saying. 'You should be able to rope the adult and pull her out with the Jeep.'

'We might have to dig round her feet first. Over,' said Anton.

'You're probably right,' said Sipho, 'but you need to take a look for yourself. Can you get down here, or are you too busy? Over.'

'No – nothing much is happening here. We'll come down. I'll have to round up the team first and load some equipment, so we could be a while getting there. Over and out,' said Anton.

Mandy was elated. 'Great,' she cried excitedly. 'Did you hear that, Levina?' she called across to Levina who was still relaxing against the fever tree.

'Only bits of it,' answered Levina, 'I think I must have dozed off for a minute.'

'Anton's coming to rescue the giraffe. He said they'd dig out round her feet and then pull her out of the mud with the jeep,' Mandy said, jumping down from the Land-rover.

'Sounds tricky,' said James.

'It sounds as if *you* hope it'll be too tricky for it to work,' said Mandy to him irritably. She had to believe that everything would go smoothly. '*I* think it's all going to work out,' she said to him confidently.

'Let's hope so,' James muttered, turning away from Mandy and walking back to the fever tree.

'Yes, let's all hope for the best,' said Levina in a soothing tone. 'But you must be prepared for the worst, too, Mandy. There's no guarantee that the rescue will be successful. And don't forget what we were saying earlier about injuries.'

Mandy went across to Levina and sat on the ground next to her. 'If she *is* injured, but not seriously, you'd still take her back to the base, wouldn't you?' she asked hesitantly.

'As long as the injuries were superficial and required very little treatment and not too much of my time, then we'd take her back,' Levina said.

'I'm sure Mum and Dad would help,' Mandy said quickly. 'Then it wouldn't have to take up too much of your time. And I would do anything you wanted me to do to help out,' she added eagerly. She felt that anything that would make things easier for Levina would be in the giraffes' favour.

'That would certainly be a big help,' said Levina.

'But let's wait until I've got some idea of the condition of the giraffe before we make any firm plans.'

Sipho and Lindiwe joined them. 'A bit congested here!' laughed Sipho, 'You and I will have to move to the next tree, Lindiwe, if we want a place to rest!'

'I'll come with you,' said James, scrambling up from the ground. 'How long will they take to get here?' he asked Sipho.

'About two hours, I guess,' said Sipho.

'So long?' asked Mandy. She was desperate for the giraffe's ordeal to end soon. The longer she remained in the mud, the greater the risk that she would become too exhausted for Levina to treat.

'They need some time to sort out their equipment,' explained Sipho, 'and then, remember, it took us more than an hour to get here. We must be patient. Like the giraffe. See, she has become resigned to her trap – she no longer fights to escape it.'

Mandy noticed that the giraffe had stopped struggling. It looked as if she had accepted her fate. Mandy wished there were some way they could reassure her that help was close at hand. All they could do now was wait and hope for the best.

# *Five*

'Well, since we're going to be here for a while, why don't we have something to eat?' suggested Levina.

'Good idea,' said James eagerly. 'I'll get the cool box.'

James slipped his camera and binoculars from round his neck and handed them to Levina. Then he and Lindiwe fetched the cool box and a large insulated jug of iced orange juice from the Land-rover.

'Let's use this as a table,' suggested Lindiwe, placing the jug on a large, flat rock in the shade of the fever tree where Levina and Mandy were sitting.

Everyone clustered round the makeshift picnic table and helped themselves to sandwiches, while Lindiwe poured out juice. Mandy took a half-hearted bite of an avocado sandwich, but she didn't feel like eating She watched James tucking into his sandwich and wondered how he and the others could even think of food.

'Who would like some biltong?' asked Sipho, taking a pack of strange-looking dried meat out of the cool box.

'I'll try some,' said James, accepting a chunk of it from Sipho.

'Anyone else?' asked Sipho.

Mandy pulled a face. As the others sat eating contentedly, it struck her that they were perfectly happy with their place at the top of the food chain. She put her uneaten sandwich on the rock.

'Aren't you hungry?' James asked.

'No,' Mandy replied abruptly.

James looked bewildered. He pushed his glasses up his nose, blinked and then reached for his mug of juice.

Mandy looked across to the waterhole. Apart from a few doves sipping at the edge of the water, nothing had changed. She looked at her watch. Half an hour had passed since Sipho had spoken to Anton. She decided she'd try not to think about the giraffe waiting to be rescued. If she concentrated on other things it might help to make the waiting more bearable. She took a few steps forward and surveyed the surrounding area through her binoculars to see if she could spot any animals, but the bush looked deserted.

After a while, she went back to sit next to Levina under the fever tree. Everyone had finished eating and Sipho was packing away the remains of the picnic. 'Anyone like to come for a walk?' he asked after he'd put the cool box and jug back in the Land-rover.

'Yes, please!' Mandy grabbed her baseball cap and jumped to her feet.

James collected his camera and binoculars while Lindiwe picked up her father's rifle, which he had leaned against the rock while he was eating.

Slinging his rifle across his chest, Sipho led the way down a well-used game track leading away from the waterhole. 'Keep close to me and be as quiet as antelopes,' he said. 'If we are lucky we may come across some game.'

'I just hope those lions aren't anywhere about!' remarked Levina from the back of the little procession.

'I'd like to see lions again,' murmured James, who was walking next to Mandy.

Mandy looked at him in dismay. He smiled at her, but she turned away without smiling back at him.

They picked their way cautiously along the track. A faint rustling sound in the long grass a few metres ahead of them caused them to stop dead. They waited in silence. Then a male warthog burst out of the grass, his family hot on his heels. They bustled busily across the path, hardly taking any notice of the humans, and disappeared into the grass on the other side.

James laughed quietly. 'Their tails look like radio aerials, sticking up stiffly like that,' he whispered.

Mandy smiled at the idea. A black millipede at her feet coiled itself into a tight spiral as she brushed her foot against it by mistake.

'What do you call those again?' she asked Lindiwe. A few days earlier, David Mackenzie had told her the local name but she'd forgotten it.

'*Shongololos*,' Lindiwe told her.

They walked on. Apart from the warthogs and *shongololos* there was nothing to hint at the teeming wildlife in the vastness beyond. The midday heat had temporarily subdued everything.

Sipho turned round and said, 'I think we've gone far enough. Let's go back.' He led them back to the waterhole.

Mandy looked on in astonishment as they approached the clearing. A troop of baboons had taken over the spot where they'd had their picnic. There were even a few young ones clambering over the Land-rover. Sipho ran across to the vehicle and shooed them off. As Mandy and the others caught up with him, they saw that the

baboons had managed to open the cool box.

'I'm glad we've had our lunch,' said James, as the young baboons scuttled off to catch up with the rest of the troop.

'They must have been watching us all the time we were eating,' said Levina, as they clambered back into the Land-rover and settled down to wait. 'As soon as we left, they took the chance to grab what they could.'

Mandy glanced at her watch. They'd been waiting for over an hour and a half, and both James and Levina had fallen asleep. She wondered what would happen if lions *did* appear before the rescue team arrived. Would Sipho try to scare them off or would he radio the team and tell them to turn back? She was about to ask, when she heard the sound of an engine.

'They're nearly here,' she exclaimed. 'I can hear them.'

A few minutes later the team arrived. A big green Jeep pulled up alongside the Land-rover followed by a lorry with strong bars at the back, forming a type of cage. Sipho and Mandy jumped out of the Land-rover to meet them. The noise of the arriving vehicles woke James.

'Ow, my neck!' Mandy heard him moan as he raised his head.

Stifling a laugh, she turned to him and said, 'Now you know how the giraffe feels.'

James grimaced, eased himself out of the Land-rover and stood next to Mandy, who had turned her attention to the four newcomers. She recognised Anton, and Paul, who was Sipho's deputy, but she didn't know the other two men.

'Who are they?' she whispered to Lindiwe who, with Levina, had joined the group.

'They're both game rangers,' explained Lindiwe: 'The one with the beard is Mduduzi and the other man is Bongani.'

'Right,' said Anton starting to walk off. 'Let's have a close look so we can see what to do. Are you coming, Levina?'

Levina nodded and strode after the men towards the waterhole, beckoning the others to follow. 'You can come too if you like. Just don't get too close!'

They reached the waterhole and Mandy looked anxiously at the giraffes, wondering if the approaching humans would terrify them.

Lindiwe put a hand on her arm and said quietly, 'Don't worry. Anton and his men have done this kind of thing hundreds of times. They will be careful. My father even believes that Anton can think like one of the animals he's handling.'

'Thanks,' said Mandy, smiling at Lindiwe. 'I know they must be really experienced and I can't wait to see what they're going to do, but I just can't help worrying about the giraffes – they must be so scared.' She thought the mother giraffe was looking more afraid than before.

'We should be able to get the Jeep down here without getting it stuck,' Anton was saying. 'I just need to see how deep the giraffe has sunk and how soft the mud is there. Come, Sipho, let's go and check.'

The two men walked around the edge of the waterhole and stopped close to the giraffe. The calf took fright as they drew near and trotted away to take refuge behind a nearby fever tree. Anton sat on his haunches near the hind legs of the giraffe, looking thoughtful.

'I hope the giraffe doesn't kick out now,' said James.

'How can she? She's stuck – not fit enough, remember?' Mandy knew she was being unfair but she couldn't help feeling angry with him for not supporting her earlier.

James looked hurt and turned away.

Anton and Sipho exchanged a few words then returned to the rest of the group.

'You'll be happy to know,' Sipho said, smiling broadly at Mandy, 'that Anton thinks it won't be too complicated to get the giraffe out.'

Mandy grinned at him. 'I'm *very* happy to know that' she said.

'How are you going to do it?' James asked Anton.

'Well, like I said on the radio, we're going to tie her to the side of the Jeep, then dig out round her front feet to remove as much mud as we can. That will help to dislodge her,' Anton explained. 'Then we'll drive her out.'

'Dig round her feet – that sounds dangerous!' remarked James.

'It could be, but I don't think she'll be able to move her feet until she has the power of the Jeep to assist her,' Anton said reassuringly. 'It's a bit like pulling someone out of quicksand.' He turned to his assistants. 'OK, let's get moving,' he said to them. 'I'll bring the Jeep down here. Bongani, you reverse the lorry as close as you can get it. Then you can help me to lash the giraffe to the side of the Jeep. Paul, you and Mduduzi can dig round the giraffe's hooves when she's tied to the Jeep. Sipho, you'll keep a lookout, won't you?'

Sipho nodded. He slipped his rifle back from over his shoulders and held it in both hands.

The men returned quickly to the vehicles to begin their tasks.

'I think you three should go back to the Land-rover,' said Levina. 'It'll be better if you're out of harm's way.'

'Are you staying to help?' Lindiwe asked Levina.

Levina nodded. 'Yes, I need to get some idea of the extent of her injuries.'

Mandy led the way back to the Land-rover. 'At least we've got a good view from here,' she said, climbing up on to the bull-bars at the front so that she could sit on the bonnet.

Lindiwe and James climbed up alongside her, James with his camera at the ready.

'You should get some really good pictures,' said Lindiwe. 'Not many people get a chance like this.'

James nodded, smiling at her.

'You wouldn't have had this opportunity if they'd decided to leave the giraffe to its fate,' Mandy reminded him pointedly.

'I know,' said James, not looking at her.

The rescue team swung into action. Anton edged the Jeep close to the left of the giraffe. She looked nervously at the vehicle pulling up beside her, but seemed resigned to her situation. Bongani reversed the lorry as far as he could, then he let down the wooden back to form a ramp for the giraffes to walk up.

From the safety of the fever tree, the calf watched the activity around his mother. 'He looks so confused and frightened,' Mandy murmured. 'I hope he won't run off.'

Bongani quietly moved round to the right side of the adult giraffe with a thick rope in his hands. He threw one end of the rope over the giraffe's back to Anton, who was now standing in the back of the Jeep. Up until now, the giraffe had stood motionless, but the sudden movement of the rope seemed to alarm her and she started to struggle violently, even managing to kick out with one of her back legs. Paul was standing behind her. In a split second, he leaped aside, avoiding being seriously hurt.

'That was close,' said James, breathing a sigh of relief.

The men waited for a minute while the giraffe calmed down, then Anton skilfully looped the rope under the giraffe's belly and threw it back to Bongani. As Bongani prepared to throw the rope to Anton again, the giraffe kicked out once more in a frenzy, swinging her huge neck with tremendous force and nearly banging it into the side of the Jeep. Bongani had to jump back quickly to get out of the way.

'I suppose if she can resist like that, she can't be too badly injured,' said Mandy, astonished at the strength of the exhausted giraffe.

Levina had been standing with Sipho, well away from the action. She said a few words to him then ran back to the Land-rover and pulled a small towel out of her knapsack. 'I'm going to try to calm her down,' she said to the three friends. 'It's beginning to look dangerous, so just stay where you are – don't even think about leaving the Land-rover.'

Levina ran to the Jeep and climbed into the front. The men had stopped trying to rope the giraffe. Mandy held her breath as Levina stretched across to get close to the giraffe and then began massaging it all around its shoulder area and at the base of its neck. She held her breath, waiting to see how the giraffe would react. Just one swipe of her neck could easily unbalance

Levina and make her fall. But the giraffe seemed calmed by Levina's presence. The scientist moved her hands down the giraffe's neck until she'd reached its face, then, with one hand she placed the towel over its eyes while continuing to massage with the other hand. The giraffe didn't move a muscle. Mandy let out a sigh of relief.

'That was clever of Levina,' said James.

'She's very brave,' said Lindiwe in admiration.

With the giraffe calm once more, Anton and Bongani continued harnessing her. They passed the rope round the animal's body a few more times, then Anton tied the two ends of the rope firmly to the Jeep. The giraffe was now securely lashed to the side of the vehicle.

Paul and Mduduzi had grabbed shovels from the back of the lorry and were digging round the giraffe's front hooves, scooping out the mud. Through her binoculars, Mandy watched the men working. Soon it looked as if the giraffe was standing in two large hollows. They dug deeper, close to its feet, until the giraffe's black hooves were clearly visible.

Suddenly Lindiwe whispered, 'Look – the calf – it's coming this way!'

Mandy lowered her binoculars and looked to

where Lindiwe was pointing. The calf was moving slowly towards them. He walked forward a few paces, then stopped and gazed at the Land-rover before taking a few more steps in their direction.

'He looks a lot calmer now,' Mandy said quietly.

'Mmm, he seems quite relaxed,' agreed Lindiwe.

'Maybe it's because his mother isn't upset any more,' suggested James.

'Could be,' said Lindiwe.

The calf kept moving towards them. Soon he was only a few metres away, watching them intently, his lower jaw chewing and his big, brown eyes winking alternately. Mandy couldn't help laughing softly. 'He's so inquisitive,' she said. 'It's as if he's come to inspect us.'

The young giraffe reached the Land-rover. He stared at them for a minute, then lowered his neck and started sniffing Mandy. She sat absolutely still. Then he started to 'taste' her face with his long, black tongue. It felt as if a piece of wet sandpaper was being rubbed over her face. She giggled and the calf began to lick her hair, knocking off her cap. Slowly Mandy reached out to touch his neck, but the calf backed away in alarm.

'*He*'s not ready for a massage,' whispered Lindiwe.

The calf gazed at them for a few more moments, then turned and loped towards the waterhole.

'That was amazing!' Mandy gasped.

'I wish I'd been able to take some photos,' said James. 'But I didn't want to frighten him off.'

Mandy turned her attention back to the rescue. The digging had been completed. The men had moved away from the waterhole and Anton was starting up the Jeep. He inched the vehicle forward. The giraffe lifted her neck and Anton moved the Jeep forward a few more centimeters. Mandy thought she saw the giraffe also move forward. Anton tried again. This time, the giraffe threw her neck back and, with one mighty thrust, pulled her forelegs up.

'He's done it!' Mandy cried. 'She's free!'

# *Six*

Anton drove slowly up the bank, the giraffe walking stiffly alongside. He stopped by the lorry, and the calf trotted over to greet his mother. She reached back with her neck as he began to suckle.

Levina got out of the Jeep and walked across to the Land-rover. Mandy, James and Lindiwe jumped down to meet her.

'I thought we were going to have trouble there,' said Levina.

'You were amazing,' Mandy said warmly.

'I learned that massage technique from a physiotherapist a few months ago,' Levina explained, smiling. 'I have to admit that I wasn't sure it would work on such a distressed animal, but it was worth a try.'

'Is she OK?' asked James.

'I'm not sure yet,' Levina told her. 'We want to give her and the calf a few minutes to calm down, then I'm going to take a closer look at her. I thought I'd grab a drink in the meantime – that was thirsty work!'

'I'll pour you some juice,' offered Lindiwe, reaching for the jug.

'Thanks,' said Levina, smiling gratefully.

Levina quenched her thirst, then pulled her bag from the back of the Land-rover and produced a stethoscope.

James looked surprised. 'Do you always carry that around with you?' he asked.

'I suppose I do,' chuckled Levina. 'I like to be prepared when I'm out in the bush!' She hung the stethoscope round her neck. 'Seeing as the giraffe is firmly tied to the Jeep, I don't see why you three can't come with me.'

'I was hoping you'd say that!' Mandy beamed.

They walked down to the waterhole, where the men stood a few metres away from the two giraffes.

Sipho turned to Levina. 'Ready?' he asked.

Levina nodded.

'Do you need any help?' asked Anton.

'I don't know,' answered Levina. 'But perhaps you can sit in the Jeep, just in case I need you.'

Levina and Anton climbed into the Jeep. Levina moved carefully to the giraffe's side and stood on the front seat to reach the animal. Mandy watched the giraffe's face closely. She seemed quite peaceful now, but Mandy had learned that this could change in a split second. Levina cautiously began to massage the huge neck and shoulders once more. The giraffe stood motionless, looking straight ahead.

'Look at her expression,' said Mandy turning to Lindiwe. 'She looks blissful!'

'She *does* look as if she's smiling,' agreed Lindiwe.

Mandy fidgeted nervously as Levina, standing on the tips of her toes and leaning far forward, listened to the giraffe's heart. She watched in admiration as the scientist soothed the animal towering above her. Levina began to palpate the giraffe's chest, shoulders and upper forelegs. Mandy thought she could see the giraffe flinch every now and then. She was on tenterhooks, waiting to hear the diagnosis. She couldn't bear to think that Levina might decide that the animal needed to be destroyed.

At last, Levina turned away from the giraffe, said a few words to Anton, then climbed out of the Jeep and came back to the rest of the team.

Mandy couldn't wait for Levina to speak. She ran towards her, with James and Lindiwe following behind. 'Is she all right?' she burst out, eagerly.

Levina smiled at Mandy. 'I think she's going to be fine,' she reassured her.

Mandy sighed with relief.

'Does that mean you're going to let her go now?' asked James.

'No, I don't think so – she *is* exhausted,' replied Levina, turning to Sipho. 'The giraffe has sustained some injuries,' she told him, 'but it's nothing too dramatic. I'm pretty sure she's suffering mainly from severe bruising and muscle strain, so a spell in the *boma* will help her to recover.'

'No expensive treatment?' Sipho asked guardedly.

Levina shook her head. 'No, I don't think so – but I'd like to check her more thoroughly when we get her back to the base. I'm going to ask Adam and Emily to help me. I'm pretty sure that all she needs is a few days of complete rest,' she assured him.

'Oh, that's wonderful!' exclaimed Mandy, feeling a flood of relief. She turned to James. 'I *told* you everything would work out,' she said triumphantly.

James nodded but said nothing. Mandy wondered if he was still not convinced that rescuing the giraffes had been the right thing to do.

'Let's get them loaded into the lorry,' Anton said, clapping his hands together and striding back to the Jeep. He swung himself into the driver's seat and started up the engine.

'I think we should go back to the Land-rover and wait for Sipho,' Levina suggested to Mandy, James and Lindiwe. 'Anton can take over now – he's the capture expert.'

As they walked away from the waterhole, Mandy wondered if there'd be any trouble getting the giraffes to go up the ramp into the back of the lorry. She hoisted herself on to the Land-rover's bonnet and looked on anxiously as Anton stopped the Jeep at the foot of the ramp.

'I wonder how they're going to get her to go up

there?' mused James, who was standing on the bull-bars.

'It looks like they're going to untie her from the Jeep first,' commented Lindiwe, who was standing on the front seat next to Levina.

'You're right,' said Mandy, as she noticed Mduduzi untying the rope. Soon the giraffe was no longer lashed to the side of the Jeep, although she still wore her rope harness. Mduduzi stood on the ground, next to the giraffe, gripping the rope in both hands.

'I hope she doesn't decide to take off now,' said James.

'I think she's too bruised and stiff to do that,' Levina told them, pushing her hair back out of her eyes.

'Anyway, Bongani's going to help,' said Mandy as the other game ranger took hold of the rope as well. Together, the two men started to mount the ramp, pulling on the rope so that the giraffe would have to follow them. The men tugged and pulled. The giraffe refused to move.

'She's digging her heels in,' said Mandy, biting her fist. 'She's much stronger than them!'

She watched as Paul and Sipho stepped forward to help. The four men heaved and pulled until, gradually, the giraffe had no choice but to move forward.

'It's like a tug-of-war!' exclaimed James as the giraffe slowly walked up the ramp. He lifted his camera to take another shot of the rescue operation.

'I suppose that much of her resistance is because it hurts when she moves,' said Levina.

'I didn't think of that. Poor giraffe,' said Mandy sympathetically. 'Oh good, she's inside now.'

Mandy could see the men quickly lashing the rope to a side bar, securing the giraffe in the lorry. Then they hurried back down the ramp. 'Now what about the calf?' she wondered aloud.

The calf had followed his mother when she was driven to the foot of the ramp. He had stopped a short distance away and still stood there, sniffing the air and looking about. He glanced across at the Land-rover and for a moment seemed to look directly at Mandy.

'Go on,' she murmured, 'go up the ramp with your mother. You're going to be safe.'

The calf flicked his tail and twitched his ears nervously, then looked at his mother standing in the back of the lorry. He approached the ramp gingerly and, without so much as a backward glance, walked confidently up it.

'He must have felt reassured, seeing her standing so calmly in the lorry,' said Mandy happily. She slid down off the bonnet and climbed into the Land-rover, making room for James as he climbed in beside her. Lindiwe clambered over from the front seat and sat between them.

The capture team sprang into action once more. Paul and Bongani quickly raised the ramp and slid across the strong bolts that held it in place. They climbed into the cab of the lorry and Mduduzi joined Anton in the Jeep.

Sipho jogged over to the Land-rover. 'So far, so good,' he said, getting into the front of the vehicle. 'The next step will be to get them to go back down the ramp at the *boma*.'

The vehicles started to move out in convoy, with the Land-rover bringing up the rear. As they left the waterhole, Mandy turned to look back at the now-peaceful scene. Only a few tyre tracks and the scooped-out area where the giraffe had been stuck gave any indication of the giraffe's recent struggle for survival.

It was mid-afternoon by the time they reached the research base. David and Sophie Mackenzie were waiting at the gate of the *boma*. Mandy waved to them as the Land-rover lurched to a halt nearby.

'We've had an amazing time,' she said, as she jumped down from her seat.

'We heard! I wish I'd been there,' said David, sounding a little envious. 'Mmatsatsi told us that Anton was rescuing a giraffe. We've been waiting here quite a while – we didn't want to miss anything when you got back.'

Paul reversed the lorry slowly through the huge gates. Mandy and the others followed Sipho to wait by the open gateway to watch the proceedings.

'I can't see much,' Mandy complained, 'just the cab of the lorry and the tops of the trees. I don't suppose we could go inside?' she asked Levina hopefully. Levina raised her eyebrows.

'I've got an idea,' David said. 'Let's climb up there.' He pointed to a large tree by the *boma* fence. 'We should get a really good view.'

Mandy looked up at the tree. It looked like an easy climb, and the branches were certainly sturdy enough to carry their weight.

'Good idea,' said James enthusiastically.

'And it's safe,' said Lindiwe, looking at Sipho. '*You'd* be happier if we watched from up there, wouldn't you, *Baba*?'

Sipho smiled affectionately at his daughter. 'You know me very well!' he said.

David scaled the thick trunk, followed by Mandy, Lindiwe, James and Sophie.

'You were right,' Mandy said happily, looking up at David who was sitting on a branch above her. 'We can see everything from here.' She looked down at the lorry. Mduduzi and Bongani had opened the back, and Anton had climbed up the bars at the side of the vehicle and untied the rope that secured the adult giraffe. Mandy expected the giraffe to walk down the ramp as soon as she was free, but she didn't move.

'It looks like they're going to have to pull her out, the same way they pulled her into the lorry,' she said.

'I think you're right,' agreed Lindiwe. 'Look, Paul's going to help Anton.'

'They'll have to get her to turn first,' said David. 'She's facing the wrong way.'

Paul climbed over the bars and joined Anton. Together they began to tug at the rope. The giraffe stomped lightly on the spot where she stood, then, guided by the men, she turned and slowly stepped down the ramp with painstakingly slow, awkward movements.

'Poor thing, she's really hurting,' Mandy breathed.

'Is she going to get better?' asked Sophie, who was sharing Mandy's branch.

'Levina says she'll be fine,' said Mandy, smiling encouragingly at her. 'Oh good, the calf's coming down too,' she cried excitedly as the young giraffe clambered confidently down the ramp to join its mother at the bottom.

The adult giraffe had stopped only a few paces away from the ramp and refused to move any further. As Anton and Paul unwrapped the ropes from her body, she hardly even looked at them. She was subdued and listless.

Mduduzi raised the ramp, then he and the rest of the team clambered into the lorry and drove out of the *boma*, waving and saluting to Mandy and the others in the tree, who now started to scramble down.

'Are you going to examine the giraffe again later?' Mandy asked Levina anxiously, when she reached the ground. 'I'll go and get Mum and Dad to help you, if you like.'

'No, I think we'll call it a day now,' said Levina, yawning. 'I'm pretty tired and I think we should leave the giraffes to themselves to recover a little.

Perhaps your parents can meet me here tomorrow morning after breakfast?'

'I'll ask them,' said Mandy. She felt a little disappointed, realising she would have to wait until the morning to be sure that the giraffes really were safe.

'See you tomorrow,' called Lindiwe to her friends as she set off with Sipho and Levina in the direction of the base buildings.

Mandy waved, then followed James, David and Sophie along the protected walkway that led back to the Lodge.

# Seven

Adam and Emily Hope were sitting on the veranda outside their cabin when Mandy and James called for them at breakfast time the next morning. 'Where have you been?' asked Mr Hope, raising his eyebrows. 'We've been waiting for you for hours!'

'You *haven't*, Dad,' laughed Mandy as he rose from his chair and headed for the main building.

Inside the dining-room, they found a table and went to choose from the buffet. Mandy filled a bowl with fruit and cereal. Just as she was about to go back to the table, she noticed her father hunting amongst the cereal boxes.

'What are you looking for, Dad?' she asked.

'Cornflakes,' he said. He called to a waiter standing nearby. 'Excuse me. Are there any cornflakes?'

'Yes, sir, we put a new box out yesterday morning,' replied the waiter, hurrying across to the buffet.

Mr Hope looked puzzled. 'I can't see it,' he said.

The waiter looked at the various cereals. He moved the boxes around, then picked up each one. He stood with his chin in one hand for a few moments, staring at the boxes in front of him, then sifted through them again.

'Eh, I don't know!' he exclaimed, bending down to look under the buffet table. Mr Hope bent down too.

Mandy looked at her mother and giggled. Emily Hope shook her head. 'The lengths your father will go to for food!' she said, smiling.

Adam Hope and the waiter stood up simultaneously and bumped into each other. James burst out laughing, almost spilling the cereal in his bowl.

The waiter shrugged his shoulders and pulled a face, 'I cannot understand,' he said. 'I put them here myself – a new box!' Baffled, the waiter indicated the spot where'd he left them. '*Hau*, I am very confused!'

A waitress arrived to see what was going on, and began an animated discussion with her colleague. Then she bustled out of the dining-room, looking thoroughly bemused.

'See what you've done,' whispered Emily, smiling at her husband who was sheepishly pouring a different cereal into his bowl.

They returned to their table and had just started to eat when the waitress reappeared with Lindiwe's mother, Mmatsatsi Ngomane, who worked in the hotel office. Mmatsatsi looked around, said a few words to the staff, then greeted Mandy and her family.

'Good morning,' she said to them cheerfully, 'I'm sorry about the cornflakes, Mr Hope. I've sent for another box.'

'Oh dear,' said Adam Hope, sounding embarrassed. 'I'm sorry, I seem to have caused an awful fuss.'

'You know, it's odd,' said Emily Hope after Mmatsatsi had left. 'A couple of things have gone missing from our suite too – that string of beads I bought at the shop the other day and the chain for my sunglasses.'

'And I couldn't find one of my scrunchies,' said Mandy, peeling an orange. 'Oh, I've just remembered! I saw a box of cornflakes on the ground outside yesterday morning when we were on our way to meet Levina and Sipho.'

James put his spoon down and looked at Mandy. 'And my cashew nuts went missing,' he said thoughtfully. 'Remember? I couldn't find them yesterday.'

'It all seems very strange,' said Mr Hope, leaning back in his chair 'I wonder if there's a thief on the loose?' He pushed his cereal bowl to one side. 'I think I'll see if they've left us any eggs!'

Mandy felt agitated as James and her father tucked into their cooked breakfast. She wanted to get to the *boma*. After what seemed an age, they had finally eaten enough. Mandy pushed back her chair and stood up quickly. 'At last!' she said. 'Let's go.'

Levina was already at the *boma* along with David and Lindiwe when they arrived.

'Hi, everybody,' said Lindiwe, running over to meet them. 'Levina said we can go into the *boma* when they examine the mother,' she told them enthusiastically.

'That's great!' Mandy beamed. She had been hoping they'd be allowed to get a bit closer to the giraffes today.

'Hi, Levina,' said Emily Hope.

Mr Hope raised a hand in greeting. 'What's the procedure?' he asked.

'Let's go in and take a look,' Levina said, gesturing towards the gate in the fence. 'Mandy, James and Lindiwe should be quite safe if they stay near the gate,' she said, picking up her bag.

One by one, they stepped cautiously through the gate. The giraffes were standing close together, the calf suckling from its mother – but they were still in the same spot as the evening before.

'It looks like the mother hasn't moved at all,' she said anxiously.

David agreed. 'Maybe it's because she *can't* move. Or because she's weak from hunger.'

Levina watched the giraffes. 'I'm sure the mother will let us approach her,' she said. 'She looks quite calm.'

Levina and Mr and Mrs Hope made their way slowly towards the giraffes. As they got closer, the calf sidled off, but the mother hardly twitched a muscle. Levina stood below the giraffe's chest and stretched up to soothe her. Mandy could see that Levina was straining to reach the giraffe. 'She needs something to stand on,' she said.

'There's an empty crate outside the gate,' suggested Lindiwe, 'the sort they use for transporting smaller animals. She could stand on that.'

Mandy and Lindiwe went to fetch the crate, and carried it back into the *boma*.

Mandy waited until her father turned round. She pointed to the crate and then to Levina. Adam Hope nodded and beckoned to her.

'Come on, let's take it to them,' she whispered to Lindiwe.

James stepped forward and reached for the crate, 'Need some help?' he asked hopefully.

'No thanks, we can manage,' Mandy replied. She and Lindiwe made their way carefully towards Levina.

'Thanks, you two,' said Levina quietly as they positioned the crate on the ground beneath the giraffe's chest. Close up, Mandy could appreciate the power and strength of the magnificent animal. She noticed the bulging muscles in its upper legs and could understand how it was possible for a giraffe to outrun a lion.

Mandy stepped back and stood with Lindiwe a few metres away.

'She's amazing,' Mandy breathed, looking up at the giraffe. She glanced across to James and David standing next to the fence.

Mr and Mrs Hope examined the animal while Levina kept her calm. The giraffe looked peaceful and she stood patiently as the humans felt the muscles in her chest, neck and legs and listened to her heart.

'It's as if she knows they want to help her,' Lindiwe smiled.

At last, the vets moved away from the animals, and Mandy waited for the verdict.

'Well, I agree with you, Levina,' said Adam Hope. 'Just severe muscle strain and bruising, wouldn't you say, Emily?'

'Yes, I can't find anything else to worry about,' his wife said. 'She'll be as right as rain in a few days.'

'That's wonderful,' said Mandy, grinning at her mother.

Mr Hope picked up the crate and they walked back to David and James by the gate.

'She's going to be fine,' Mandy told them.

'Doesn't she need any treatment?' asked David,

as they left through the small gate.

'There's nothing much we can do, really,' Levina told him. 'She'll recover after a few days' rest.' She turned to Mr and Mrs Hope who were following just behind, 'We *could* try rubbing her with some arnica ointment, if she'll let us. I've got a big tub of it in my office.'

'What's arnica?' asked James.

'It's an ointment made from a plant – it's useful for bruises,' Emily Hope explained. She turned to her husband. 'I think that's a job we can take over,' she said to him. 'Then Levina can get on with her other work.'

Levina smiled gratefully.

'No problem,' agreed Mr Hope, putting the crate down. 'We'll come to your office after lunch and pick up the arnica. Turning to Mandy and her friends he added, 'And you four could help collect some food.'

'Really?' asked Mandy, keen to help in any way she could.

'There are only one or two thorn trees in the *boma*,' Levina told them. She pointed through the open gate. 'It would really help,' she continued, pulling the gate shut and fastening the padlock, 'if you could collect acacia branches to feed them.'

'Great!' said Mandy. 'When can we start?'

'How about now?' suggested David.

'Where will we get the branches?' asked James, looking doubtfully at the area surrounding the *boma*. 'There aren't many acacia trees out here either,' he said.

'I'll ask Sipho if you can go out a little way into the reserve with a ranger every day,' said Levina, hanging her bag over her shoulder. 'In the meantime, I'm sure David's mum and dad won't mind if you gather some from the trees in the Lodge grounds – as long as you don't make it look as if a whole herd has been on the rampage!' She glanced at her watch. 'I've got to get back to the office. I'll see you after lunch, Emily and Adam,' she said, moving off towards the base.

'Yes, time to get back to the pool,' said Adam Hope with an exaggerated sigh.

'And time for the giraffes to be fed,' said Mandy as they all set off for the walkway.

Back at the Lodge, Mandy's parents headed for the pool and Mandy and the others started to look for suitable trees.

'There are some acacias at the back of the kitchen,' said David, leading the way.

'I think we ought to name the giraffes,' Mandy

suggested as they followed him across the neat lawns of Ubungane Lodge.

'OK,' agreed David. 'What about Tall and Short?'

'Or Patches and Blotches?' suggested Lindiwe.

'That's a nice idea,' said Mandy.

'How about Little and Large?' James offered.

Mandy shook her head. 'I know! Let's call the calf Lucky and the mother Chance – because of the lucky chance they had escaping from the lions.'

'Lucky and Chance! Perfect!' said Lindiwe enthusiastically. David and James nodded in agreement as they rounded the kitchen building. Ahead of them stood a small clump of thorn trees.

'Let's get to work,' said David, breaking a thin branch off a low tree. Mandy and the others followed his example, breaking off twigs and shoots that were within their reach.

'Ouch!' cried Mandy, catching her hand on a sharp thorn. She paused and sucked at the cut on her hand, then continued gathering food for Lucky and Chance. It was much harder work than she had expected, but Mandy didn't mind.

'We really need to get the new twigs and shoots

higher in the trees,' said David, pausing to look up at the tops of the trees. 'There's not much down here.'

'You have to be a giraffe to reach those,' James said, straining to break a thick branch.

'I'll get a ladder and something for cutting,' said David, looking up into a tree, 'then I'll climb up and cut down some of those thinner branches up there.'

David soon returned with a ladder, some pruning shears and a big sheet of sacking.

'I'll climb the ladder and cut off the twigs. You can pile them on to the sacking,' explained David. 'When there's enough, we'll drag the sacking to the *boma*.'

They worked for nearly an hour before Mandy looked down at the pile of branches on the sackcloth and said, 'I think we've probably got enough for now.'

They each grabbed an edge of the sackcloth and dragged it through the Lodge grounds towards the base.

Back at the *boma*, they met Sipho and Paul.

'Hi, *Baba*,' said Lindiwe. 'Look, we've got lots of branches.'

'Just in time,' said Sipho. 'We've just finished fixing up a tall trough for the mother so she can feed easily. Let's go in and put your branches on it.'

Paul opened the large gates so they could drag the sheet of branches inside. The feeding trough stood in the centre of the enclosure, close to Chance. Lucky was standing a little way off, flicking his tail as he watched them coming into the *boma*. Mandy noticed a few brown birds clambering about on Chance, pecking at her coat with their red beaks.

'Are those ox-peckers?' she asked.

'Yes – redbilled ox-peckers – they're eating ticks from her coat,' answered Sipho.

James laughed. 'Even here the giraffes can't get away from the food chain,' he said.

Mandy shot him a disapproving glance. She still hadn't really forgiven James for not supporting her in asking Sipho to save the giraffes.

It didn't take long for the six of them to pack the branches into the trough. When they'd finished, Sipho said they should leave immediately.

'But we want to watch them eating,' protested Mandy, disappointed.

'The giraffes won't eat if we stand here and watch,' explained Sipho, leading the way. He bolted the gate behind them. Then he and Paul went back to the main building of the base.

'Let's sit up in the tree while they're feeding,' suggested Mandy. 'They won't notice us up there if we choose the right branches.'

They scaled the tree and sat very still, waiting for the giraffes to make a move towards the branches. Chance showed no interest in the food but gazed sadly into the distance.

'I don't understand it,' whispered Mandy. 'I thought giraffes loved acacia.'

'They do,' said David. 'I think Chance is still a bit shocked. When she gets used to the *boma* she'll probably start eating like mad. Then it'll be a job trying to get enough food for her! Do you know how much an adult giraffe eats?'

'I think it's about fifty kilos a day,' said Lindiwe. 'That's what my dad told me.'

'Fifty kilos!' echoed James. 'That's a lot of branches to have to collect!'

'Well, I don't mind collecting them,' said Mandy, beginning her descent. 'But I suppose they'd much rather eat from real trees.'

'I don't know,' said David, as they reached the

ground. 'When Chance is walking again, we'll find out. We might get here one morning and see that the two acacia trees in the *boma* have been stripped bare!'

Lindiwe and James jumped down next to Mandy and David.

'Why don't we go back to the Lodge for a swim before lunch?' suggested David

'Good plan,' grinned James, pushing back his floppy brown fringe. 'I'm all hot from getting the branches.'

'I'm coming back this afternoon with Mum and Dad, though,' said Mandy as they set off for the Lodge, 'I want to see if the arnica massage helps Chance.'

After lunch, Mandy and James went with Mr and Mrs Hope to fetch the arnica ointment, and then headed for the *boma*. Inside the enclosure, Lucky was suckling from his mother but he instantly lifted his head as the humans entered.

'We mustn't startle them,' said Mrs Hope, leading the way. 'We still can't be sure how she'll react to our presence.'

They took a few steps in the giraffes' direction and as they did so, Lucky spun round and trotted off to the far side of the *boma*.

'He's pretty nervous,' said Mr Hope, 'but that's probably just as well.'

'Stand back for a bit while we place the crate,' Mrs Hope said to Mandy and James. 'We need to make sure she's not going to lunge away. When we're ready, you can pass me the arnica, Mandy.'

Mr Hope positioned the crate beneath the enormous animal's forequarters. Chance gazed steadily ahead.

'I think she's getting used to us,' said Mandy quietly, as she lifted the lid of the tub of arnica. She looked at the clear gel inside. It didn't look or smell medicinal. She wondered if it would do any good.

Emily Hope stepped on to the crate while her husband put his hand on one of Chance's front legs and gently rubbed his fingers over the tight skin.

'OK,' said Mrs Hope quietly. 'Pass me the arnica, Mandy.'

Mandy climbed up next to her mother and held out the tub. Mrs Hope took a large dollop of the gel and began to rub it into Chance's muscles.

'I'll rub some into her legs,' said Mr Hope, reaching up to take some of the ointment.

Mandy looked up at Chance. The giraffe looked relaxed, and Mandy was sure she appreciated the soothing massage. 'Can I rub some in?' she asked quietly.

'I don't see why not,' said Emily Hope, scooping out more of the gel. 'We've got a big area to cover, so another pair of hands will help!' She looked at James. 'Would you like to massage the other leg?' she asked.

'Yes, please,' James said enthusiastically, stepping forward and helping himself to the arnica gel.

Following her dad's example, Mandy reached up and gently rubbed the gel around one of Chance's huge knees. Chance seemed to accept her touch and didn't flinch at all. Mandy gazed up at the gentle giant, feeling privileged to be allowed to come so close. 'Thank you,' she whispered softly.

# *Eight*

Next morning, Mandy was up early. James was still asleep when she slipped quietly out of the door and ran straight to the *boma*. She was desperate to see if the arnica had made a difference. There was no one around, so she climbed the tree, half expecting to see Chance standing passively where she had been the day before. Mandy looked around. At first she couldn't see the giraffes, but she did notice that the feeding trough had been disturbed.

Then she spotted Chance and Lucky. They were partially hidden by a thorn tree and stood munching its leaves. A huge rush of relief washed over Mandy as she watched them pulling at the young shoots. She watched for a little while, then slid back down the tree. She wanted to share the good news with someone.

As Mandy raced round a bend in the walkway, she almost crashed into David Mackenzie coming the other way. 'Guess what!' she cried, taking a few steps backward to get her balance.

'What?' he asked, looking puzzled.

'Chance has moved and she and Lucky are eating!' Mandy told him excitedly. 'Come and see.'

'Great!' exclaimed David and they ran back to the tree.

Chance was still moving very slowly and stiffly.

'But at least she *is* walking,' said Mandy. 'The arnica rub must have done some good.'

'We're going to have to start collecting a lot of branches now,' said David. 'Look how much they've already stripped from those two acacias.'

'You're right,' said Mandy. 'Oh, here comes Levina.' She waved to Levina who was walking towards them from the base.

'How are they?' Levina called up to them as she reached the bottom of the tree.

'Much better,' Mandy replied. 'They're moving

about and eating.' She eased herself off her branch and climbed back down.

'Excellent!' said Levina, as Mandy reached ground level. 'Sipho has arranged for Bongani to take you out in the lorry later to collect some more branches. Just as well – those thorn trees in the *boma* won't last long, now that Chance has got her appetite back!'

'That's what David said too,' laughed Mandy, as David joined them.

'We probably won't need to apply the arnica again,' said Levina, unlocking the small gate and peering at the giraffes. 'We'll just let nature take its course and let Chance mend on her own. Much safer for us too!'

Levina closed and locked the gate. 'Right, I'm off to have some breakfast,' she announced.

'Me too,' said Mandy, heading for the walkway.

'And me,' said David, 'I'm as hungry as a giraffe!'

Over the next few days, Mandy, James, Lindiwe and David went out every morning with Bongani to gather food for the giraffes. Mandy loved going into the bush and seeing antelope, zebras and warthogs as they gathered the branches.

Lucky and Chance had come to accept the presence of the humans but still kept well back when anyone entered the *boma*. But as soon as they left the enclosure, the giraffes always went straight to the feeding trough. Mandy was sure she had been right to beg Sipho to save them, and she still found it hard to forgive James for not taking her side about the rescue.

On the fourth morning, while they were collecting branches, James cut his hand on an acacia thorn which ripped deep into his skin.

'It looks very sore,' Lindiwe said, looking concerned.

Mandy looked at the cut. It *did* look painful.

'It's not too bad,' said James, continuing to load branches into the lorry.

'But it's bleeding,' said Lindiwe. 'You should clean it and cover it.'

'Mum will have something,' said Mandy. 'Why don't we drop James at the Lodge on our way back to the *boma*?' she suggested.

James protested, but eventually he agreed to being dropped off at the Lodge. 'I'll just wash my hands and get a plaster from your mum, Mandy,' he said as he jumped out of the back of the lorry.

'Then I'll come straight to the *boma* to help with the branches.'

They drove right inside the *boma* and Bongani reversed the lorry up to the feeding trough so they could offload the branches. As Mandy, David and Lindiwe began to pile branches into the trough, Mandy noticed Lucky ambling slowly towards them.

'Look!' she whispered, standing still, her arms full of twigs.

Slowly the giraffe calf came closer. His bottom jaw chewed steadily and he flicked his tail. He stopped a few metres away and gazed at them – just as he had done when he approached the Land-rover. Mandy hardly dared to breathe. The calf leaned his long neck forward and began to sniff at the air around her.

Just then, there was a noise behind her and Lucky bolted off in alarm. Mandy turned to see James entering the *boma*.

'Now look what you've done,' she said furiously. She had come so close to being able to touch Lucky.

'I'm sorry,' James said, looking confused.

'Couldn't you see Lucky was coming to us?' Mandy demanded, as she dumped the branches on the feeder.

'No, I didn't notice – not until the last minute, and then it was too late,' he said apologetically, fiddling with his glasses.

'Well, he'll never do that again,' said Mandy, storming straight past James and out of the *boma*.

Just outside the main building, she met Levina.

'Hi,' Levina said, smiling. 'I'm just going to the *boma*. We need to decide whether Chance is fit enough to be released yet. Are you coming?'

Mandy was taken by surprise. Somehow she hadn't expected the giraffes to be released yet. 'OK,' she said.

When they got back to the base, James, Lindiwe and David had already left. Mandy and Levina entered the *boma* and watched in silence from the gate as Chance and Lucky browsed peacefully at the feeding trough. Lucky looked up. He stared at Mandy and Levina. Then, without hesitation, the calf walked directly across to them. He stopped in front of Mandy and at once began to sniff and lick her. His rough black tongue rasped across her cheek and neck.

Mandy froze for a moment but then couldn't resist reaching up to stroke his neck. This time he didn't shy away. Mandy could hardly believe her

luck! For a moment or two, Lucky stood still while Mandy stroked him. Then, without ceremony, he walked off back to his mother.

'Well, that *was* a surprise,' said Levina, looking astonished. 'But he's getting too tame for his own good. Just as well his mother looks fit again – they need to be returned to the bush before the calf gets too used to us.'

Mandy watched Lucky nuzzling against Chance. 'When are you going to release them?'

'Tomorrow, I think,' said Levina. 'I'll make the arrangements with Sipho this evening.'

Just then, a voice called softly to them from outside the *boma*: 'Can I come in?' Mandy turned to see James standing at the gate, a wistful expression on his face.

'Hi, James, come and join us,' replied Levina.

'Lucky came over to us!' Mandy told him excitedly.

'Oh!' breathed James. 'Did he let you touch him?'

Mandy nodded.

'You were lucky!' he said. 'I came to ask if you wanted to come for a swim. Your mum's waiting for us on the sundeck. And she said to tell you that there's going to be a display of traditional dancing after dinner tonight.'

'Thanks,' said Mandy, 'but I want to stay here with the giraffes for a while. They're going to be released tomorrow.'

'Oh,' said James, again. He looked down and kicked at the ground. 'I think I'll go back then. See you later, Levina.'

But Mandy wasn't able to stay with the giraffes for long, as Levina needed to get back to her office.

'Good luck, you two,' Mandy called to the giraffes as they left the *boma*. She wandered slowly back towards the Lodge. She was glad that everything had worked out so well but also felt a tinge of sadness at having to say goodbye to Lucky and Chance. She would miss them.

As Mandy reached the end of the passageway where it opened into the Lodge grounds, she noticed someone lying on the ground ahead of her. As she drew nearer, she realised it was James. He was clutching his ankle, his face creased up in pain.

'What's wrong, James?' she cried, running towards him.

'Snake!' James gasped, his eyes full of panic. 'A snake bit me!'

Mandy was stunned. For a moment she couldn't think what to do.

'A snake! Are you sure?' she asked, looking nervously around and then back to James. 'Where did it bite you?'

James lifted his hand so that Mandy could clearly see two puncture marks on his ankle.

Mandy remembered the poisonous puff adder they had seen earlier in the week. Surely James couldn't have been bitten by a puff adder?

'Wait there, I'm going to get Mum and Dad,' she told him.

'No!' James reached for her arm. 'Don't leave me alone.'

'But I have to get help,' she said, standing up. Mandy could see that James was afraid. He looked pale and his breaths were coming in short gasps. She bent down again and put her arms round him. 'I *have* to get help,' she said, trying to sound confident. 'I'm going to find Mum – she'll know what to do. I'll be really quick.'

'I'm scared,' James admitted.

'I know, but you must keep calm,' Mandy told him. 'Just lie as still as you can. I'll be back very soon, I promise.'

Mandy raced back to the Lodge, her heart thumping in her chest. She made straight for the deck and was relieved to see that her mum and dad were still there, leaning over the railings looking through their binoculars at a herd of elephants drinking and splashing in the river below.

Mandy dashed over and tugged at her mother's arm. 'Mum, Mum, you have to come quickly!' she cried urgently.

'What's wrong, Mandy?' Emily Hope asked,

still watching the elephants.

'It's James – he's been bitten by a snake!' Mandy told her.

Mandy's parents both spun round to face her.

'Where is he?' Mr Hope asked anxiously.

'Near the walkway,' said Mandy. 'You've got to come and look at him, quickly!'

'I'll just run for my first-aid kit,' Emily Hope decided efficiently. 'I'll meet you there, Mandy.'

'And I'll get Mmatsatsi to call a doctor,' said Mandy's dad, heading off for the hotel reception.

Mandy dashed back to James. He was ashen-faced and wincing in pain. She sat next to him on the ground and put her arms round his shoulders. 'Don't worry, James,' she said comfortingly, 'Mum's coming – she'll look after you. And Mmatsatsi's calling for a doctor.'

James smiled weakly.

Mandy looked again at the puncture marks on James's ankle. Around the wound, the skin was red and bruised. Mandy willed her mum to hurry up.

When Emily Hope arrived, she placed the end of her stethoscope on James's chest and listened to his breathing.

'Mmmm, not too bad,' she said. 'I'm going to

check your pulse.' She put two fingers on his wrist and sat looking at her watch for a minute. 'That's not too bad either, James,' she reassured him. 'Now, let's have a look at the bite.'

Mandy held her breath while her mother examined the bite. 'It does look nasty,' Mrs Hope said, 'but don't worry, James, we'll get you sorted out.'

At last Mandy's dad arrived. 'Hello, Adam,' said Mrs Hope. 'Come and help me get James upright.' She shuffled round to make room. 'We have to make sure that the bite is lower than your heart to reduce the absorption of poison into your system,' she told James.

Mr Hope gently raised James into a sitting position. Mandy stood miserably to one side, wishing she could be more useful. If only she hadn't been so angry with James when he had come to the *boma*. Then he would have stayed with her while she spent those last few minutes with the giraffes and he wouldn't have been bitten.

'Why don't we carry him to his room?' suggested Adam Hope. 'You'd be more comfortable in the shade, wouldn't you, James?'

James nodded weakly.

'OK, I'm going to lift you. All right?' Mr Hope said.

He eased James gently into his arms. 'That's it. Just relax and keep your leg dangling like that. Mandy, could you run to Mmatsatsi and tell her to ask the doctor to go straight to Leela's Lodge when she arrives?'

Mandy ran off towards the reception again. She arrived at Mmatsatsi's office panting hard.

'You're in a hurry, Mandy!' observed Mmatsatsi, as Mandy paused to catch her breath.

'My dad said would you send the doctor to our room, please,' gasped Mandy, leaning on the desk to catch her breath.

'I'll tell her when she gets here, but you didn't have to run to tell me this. It'll be a while before she arrives,' explained Mmatsatsi.

Mandy stared at Mmatsatsi in horror. 'But James needs her *now*. He's in danger!' she exclaimed.

'Why do you think he is in danger?' asked Mmatsatsi, calmly.

'He *must* be – a snake bit him!' Mandy replied. 'And it's all my fault!' She was fighting back the tears as she spoke, wishing she hadn't been so unkind to her best friend over the last few days.

'Now you wait a minute,' said Mmatsatsi, coming

out from behind the desk and hugging Mandy tightly to her. 'How can it be your fault?'

'It just *is*,' said Mandy unhappily. 'I'm so worried, Mmatsatsi.' She sniffed. 'James is my best friend and I was so horrible to him. I wish I hadn't been so stupid,' she sighed.

'Did you two have a fight?' asked Mmatsatsi, guiding Mandy to a chair.

'Not a fight really,' said Mandy, 'I've just been annoyed with him ever since we rescued the giraffes.'

She told Mmatsatsi how James had disagreed with her when she had wanted Sipho to save the giraffes. 'He thought we should just leave them. I was really mad at him because I wanted the giraffes to be rescued and he thought we shouldn't interfere. And now I wish I hadn't been so angry,' she finished tearfully.

'Do you know, Mandy, I think you are learning something very important,' said Mmatsatsi mysteriously.

'Am I?' Mandy was doubtful.

Mmatsatsi nodded. 'My grandmother used to tell us that in the darkness of the night, when there was a big storm, the lightning came to show us the way – even though the lightning was a terrible and dangerous force.'

'Oh,' said Mandy, feeling confused.

'You and James were caught in a dark storm,' Mmatsatsi went on. 'You were lost and could not see ahead in the darkness – you knew only the place where you were standing. And then the lightning struck close to you and you could see. The dangerous power in the lightning has helped you to see your way in the storm.'

Mandy listened carefully. Gradually, she began to understand. 'I think you're saying that the storm was when I was cross with James and I could only see my point of view. I couldn't see what James could see,' she said thoughtfully.

'That's right,' said Mmatsatsi. 'And what do you think the lightning is?'

'It must be the snake bite – the danger of it has helped me to see something clearly,' said Mandy.

'And what is it that you can now see?' asked Mmatsatsi.

'That it doesn't matter if someone thinks about things in a different way. It's silly to spoil a friendship, just because you have different opinions,' Mandy told her.

Mmatsatsi smiled broadly, 'You have learned a wise thing today, Mandy,' she said. 'Now you need to go back to your friend. I'm sure he'll be fine. You'll see.'

'Thanks,' said Mandy gratefully, as she headed for the door. 'I'll tell James I'm sorry. And I'll tell him your story too!'

When Mandy got back to Leela's Lodge, she found James propped up in his bed with his leg hanging over the side. Levina had arrived with a book about snakes, which she was showing to James.

'Well, can you remember what colour it was?' Levina asked insistently. 'You see, James, if we can identify what kind of snake it was, then we will know how best to treat you,' she explained gently.

'I'm not sure.' James sounded frustrated. 'Maybe it was brown. I didn't see it properly.'

Mandy was relieved to hear her friend talking. She had half expected to find him lying unconscious.

'Where have you been, Mandy?' asked her mother, glancing over towards her. 'You've been gone ages.'

'I was just talking to Mmatsatsi,' answered Mandy. 'She said the doctor is on her way.' She kneeled on the floor next to James. 'You're going to be just fine,' she told him confidently.

James smiled, 'I'm glad you're here, Mandy,' he told her. 'I thought you weren't speaking to me.'

'Of course I'm speaking to you,' she grinned. 'You're my best friend.'

# *Nine*

There was a knock at the door of Leela's Lodge and Mmatsatsi ushered in a young woman whom she introduced as Dr Fraser.

'Hello, James.' The doctor smiled. 'Let's have a good look at you.'

Dr Fraser checked James's breathing and pulse rates, just as Mrs Hope had done earlier. 'Well, that's all quite normal,' she said. 'Now, let's have a look at the wound.'

The doctor kneeled down on the polished floor beside the bed. Mandy watched as she unwrapped the bandage and inspected the bite on James's ankle. He flinched as she gently felt all around the fang marks.

'I'm sorry, James,' said the doctor. 'It hurts, doesn't it? The snake certainly got a good hold of you. But it's good news.'

'Am I going to be all right?' asked James cautiously.

'Of course you are,' said Dr Fraser cheerfully. 'Fortunately, I don't think the snake's venom was poisonous.'

'It wasn't?' exclaimed James. Then he added, 'It wasn't a puff adder after all, then!'

'Definitely not!' Dr Fraser laughed.

'How can you tell?' asked Mandy, curiously.

Dr Fraser moved aside to let Mandy see James's ankle. 'Have a look at the wound,' she said. 'There's not much swelling or discolouration around the bite.'

Mandy peered closely at James's ankle. There was only a little redness around the bite.

'Poisonous venom has a very visible effect,' continued the doctor. 'If you *had* been bitten by a dangerous snake, James, your whole lower leg would be very swollen by now and would have turned black or purple. And when I touched the wound, you'd have done more than just wince if it had been a serious bite!'

Mandy felt all the worry drain right out of her. Mmatsatsi had been right – James wasn't in danger. She smiled at him and he gave her a broad grin. He looked better already!

'And even if it had been a more serious, poisonous bite,' Dr Fraser told them, 'the prompt manner in which James was treated would have made a big difference.'

'We can thank Mandy for that,' said Levina. 'She was the one who found James and fetched help.'

'But it was Mum who knew what to do,' said Mandy, feeling embarrassed.

'Good teamwork, then,' said Dr Fraser. 'Now, James, can tell me exactly what happened? I may be able to work out what kind of snake it was.'

'Really?' said James, looking surprised.

'Dr Fraser isn't just a medical doctor,' explained Levina. 'She's also a herpetologist.'

'A *what*?' asked James.

'A herpetologist is someone who studies reptiles,' Levina told them. 'Dr Fraser probably knows more about snakes than anyone else in this part of the country. So you see, you're in very good hands.'

'Right, James, tell me what you remember about the snake,' said Dr Fraser, sitting down on the bed beside him.

'I didn't see it very well, but I think it was brown and quite long,' said James.

'And where were you when you were bitten?' asked the doctor.

'I was coming back from the *boma* and just where the walkway ends I heard a loud noise in that big fig tree next to the gate,' he said. 'I looked up into the tree to see what was making all the racket and I saw a flock of those huge black-and-white birds with the big beaks – what are they called again, Mandy?' asked James.

'Trumpeter hornbills?' suggested Mandy.

'Yes, that's them,' he said. 'Anyway, I was watching them hopping about the branches and rocking backwards and forwards making a sort of laughing noise when suddenly a big blob of bird droppings landed on my glasses.' He wrinkled up his nose at the memory.

Mandy started to laugh, picturing James temporarily blinded by a white coating on his glasses.

James began to laugh too and had to wipe his eyes before continuing with his story.

'I took off my glasses to clean them. The tree has a huge trunk, so I sort of moved back to lean against it, but I tripped over a big root or something at the bottom of the tree,' he explained.

'It must have been that forked buttress that juts out at the base of the fig tree,' said Levina, nodding. 'Then what happened?'

James winced. 'That's when I got bitten. It was like a sharp stab in my ankle and I fell down,' he told them. 'I saw the snake, but only for a second because it disappeared down a hole next to the trunk.'

Dr Fraser picked up Levina's snake book and flicked through it until she found the picture she was looking for.

'Do you think it looked like this one?' she asked, pointing to a long, light brown snake.

'It could have,' said James. 'But I didn't get to see it properly – I didn't have my glasses on!' he reminded her.

Mandy stifled a giggle.

'I'm willing to bet it was this snake,' said the doctor. 'It's a common mole snake, and it's quite widespread in this area. It lives in a burrow, and I think what probably happened is that when you tripped over the buttress, James, you cornered the snake and prevented it from getting to its burrow. These snakes will strike aggressively if they're cornered, but luckily they're not venomous. So the fright you got was much worse than the bite! You'll recover in no time at all.'

'Does that mean I can get up now?' James asked eagerly. 'Can I go and see Lucky and Chance?'

'You really *are* back to normal,' laughed Adam Hope. 'Animals first, as always!'

'Not so fast, James,' said the doctor. 'You've had a bad shock so I think you ought to rest for an hour or two. And there's going to be a nasty bruise on your ankle for a few days so you'll have to take it easy – no wild parties or anything!'

James looked thoughtful for a moment and then, with a big smile on his face, said, 'Chance had bruises too – maybe I should have Levina's arnica treatment!'

Mandy laughed. 'You know, James,' she told him, 'you've shown us exactly where you fit in the food chain – just below the snake!'

James grabbed a pillow and pretended to throw it at Mandy. 'Just you wait until I'm back on my feet, Mandy Hope,' he laughed.

'Well, it looks like I'm not needed here any more,' said Dr Fraser, standing up. 'Unless, of course, a fight breaks out! Arnica will do just fine for the bruises, James. Enjoy the rest of your stay at Ubungane – just keep well away from the food chain!'

Levina and Mr and Mrs Hope invited Dr Fraser to join them for tea on the deck, while Mandy stayed with James. Mrs Hope had made them promise they would stay quietly in the room until dinner, so they decided to play a game of draughts to help to while away the time.

'I'm glad I won't be missing the traditional dancing display,' James remarked.

'Me too. But I don't think you'll be *doing* much dancing with that leg,' Mandy told him as she removed one of his draughts from the board.

James grinned. 'Thanks, Mandy, I was hoping you'd do that. Now I can take two of yours,' he said, reaching out to move his counter.

'Sneaky!' said Mandy. 'And I thought you were supposed to be in shock! Hey, what was that?' She turned towards the partition, listening.

'What?' asked James.

'That noise,' whispered Mandy. 'There it is again.'

They listened in silence. From the other side of the screen that divided their room came a series of noises – a rustling noise, a thumping, a few thuds and then more rustling.

'What is it?' whispered James, looking puzzled.

'Stay there,' Mandy told him, getting to her feet. 'I'm going to have a look.'

'Careful, Mandy,' said James. 'It could be another snake!'

Mandy tiptoed across the room and peered round the screen. The sight that greeted her was so funny that she burst out laughing.

'What is it?' asked James.

'Monkeys,' Mandy told him. 'Helping themselves to our fruit *and* one of my scrunchies!'

Caught in the act, the three furry grey looters scampered out of the open door, but not before they had grabbed bananas, grapes, and Mandy's yellow scrunchie. Clutching their spoils, the monkeys scurried off on their hind legs. It was one of the funniest things Mandy had ever seen. 'I wish you could have seen them,' she laughed as she walked back round the screen.

'I did just catch a glimpse of them,' said James. 'They looked a bit like miniature chimpanzees, running off on their back legs like that.'

A disturbance in a tree just outside James's window caught Mandy's eye. 'There they are,' she said, pointing. The two culprits were sitting high

in the tree, peeling the bananas.

'Look, that one's got your scrunchie,' said James. The little monkey had slipped a back paw through the yellow hair band and was pulling at it playfully with a front paw.

'I'm glad he's found a good use for it,' laughed Mandy. 'So *those* are the thieves that have been pinching our things!'

'Do you think they took your mum's beads and sunglasses chain?' asked James.

'Probably,' agreed Mandy. 'And maybe that's what happened to Mmatsatsi's missing cornflakes too.'

James looked puzzled. 'Why would monkeys want cornflakes?'

Mandy sat down on the end of the bed. 'I don't know, but we saw a box of cornflakes on the ground under their tree the morning we went out with Sipho and Levina, remember?' Mandy asked.

James laughed. 'I expect you're right. Funny eating habits for a monkey, though,' he said.

'Now I see why there are notices everywhere asking people not to feed them,' said Mandy.

'Yes – they help themselves anyway,' said James. 'I suppose if we fed them, they'd be in the rooms all the time. Can you imagine having a whole colony of monkeys swinging in and out of your room all day?'

'That *would* be a bit much!' agreed Mandy, smiling at her best friend. It felt good to be laughing with James again.

Emily Hope came in to check on James's ankle before dinner. She brought Levina's arnica ointment with her, which she gently massaged into his bruises. Mandy sat on the bed beside her and told her about the thieving monkeys.

'That must have been quite a sight,' said Mrs Hope, as she rebandaged James's wound.

'We think they pinched your beads and chain too,' said Mandy, passing her a safety pin.

'Quite possibly. Perhaps they liked the bright colours – I can't think of any other reason,' said her mother. 'I'll just have to make sure I put everything out of sight from now on.'

She turned back to James. 'Are you sure you're feeling well enough to come to dinner?' she asked him. 'You don't have to if you don't want to, you know.'

James looked horrified. 'I'm starving!' he said.

When they had changed their clothes, Mandy and James made their way slowly across to the *lapa*, James leaning his weight on a stick Mmatsatsi had found for him.

James sat down at the table while Mandy went to get their food from the buffet. A girl dressed in traditional Zulu costume greeted Mandy while she was standing in the queue.

'Hi, Mandy,' said the girl. 'I'm glad James is better.'

'Lindiwe!' Mandy gasped in surprise. She hadn't recognised her friend in the elaborate costume.

Lindiwe laughed. 'Do I look *that* strange?'

'No, you look fantastic.' Mandy smiled. 'But doesn't that grass skirt scratch?'

'A little, but you get used to it after a while,' Lindiwe told her. 'And when I dance, I don't even notice.'

'Are you in the show after dinner?' Mandy asked, as she began to fill her plate with salad.

'Yes – and my brother too,' Lindiwe replied. 'He's a drummer.'

'Great!' exclaimed Mandy. 'I can't wait to see you dancing. Come on, let's go and tell James.'

After dinner, all the lights in the *lapa* were switched off. For a moment there was an eerie silence and then, out of the darkness, rose the sound of a drumbeat. It started softly and slowly, then gradually grew louder and more rapid. A second drum joined in with a steady, powerful rhythm. A single spotlight illuminated the two drummers – young men dressed in animal skins, standing behind tall drums. Suddenly the floor area in front of the drummers burst into light, revealing a line of dancers who immediately caught the rhythm of the drums and began to dance.

'Look, there's Lindiwe,' Mandy whispered to James.

Mandy watched entranced, as Lindiwe performed the energetic dance. Every now and then, one of the dancers would let out a high-pitched cry that sent shivers down Mandy's spine.

As the beat of the drums grew louder and more persistent, Mandy found herself unable to resist moving in time to the rhythm. Lindiwe had danced from one end of the line to the centre. Suddenly, without warning, she stepped across to Mandy, took her by the hands and pulled her into the line of dancers.

'Just do what I do,' she said with a grin. Mandy tried to follow the steps but it was all too fast. She gave up with a laugh and stood to one side, clapping to the rhythm of the beat.

It was a wonderful evening. A perfect way, Mandy thought, to celebrate all the good things that had happened that day now that James was safe and Chance and Lucky were browsing peacefully in the safety of the *boma*. She still felt a touch of sadness at the thought of having to say a final goodbye to them the next day but she was happy that they'd soon be free again. She just wished she could get rid of the nagging fear deep within her that something would go wrong tomorrow.

# *Ten*

'Shall we see if we can find the snake's burrow?' James asked Mandy, his camera at the ready, as they neared the fig tree on their way to the *boma* early the next morning.

'Let's not!' Mandy replied, giving the tree a wide berth and hurrying through the gate into the camouflaged passageway. James was limping behind her, his ankle still bandaged from the night before.

'Hey, slow down, Mandy,' he called after her, 'I can't keep up with you.'

Mandy waited for James and her parents to catch up. 'Sorry,' she said, glancing down at

James's injured foot. 'I just wanted to spend some time with Lucky and Chance before Anton comes to load them up,' she explained.

'I'd be surprised if Anton was even out of bed yet!' exclaimed Mrs Hope, yawning, as they made their way along the sheltered walkway to the base. The dancing display had gone on late the night before.

A heavy mist hung over the *boma* and the sun was still rising in the sky. The gates of the *boma* were still locked and there was no sign of Levina or Sipho.

'I'd forgotten about the locked gates,' said Mandy, feeling disappointed. 'We'll just have to wait for Anton before we can see the giraffes.' She sat down on a rock by the *boma* fence.

'Why don't you climb the tree and watch them from there?' suggested James.

Mandy shook her head. 'You can't climb with your bad ankle. You'd be stuck down here,' she replied.

A figure emerged out of the mist. 'Lindiwe, hi!' Mandy called quietly, waving at her.

'Hi,' said Lindiwe. 'How's your ankle, James?'

'Still a bit sore,' he replied, grimacing. 'I don't think I'll be climbing trees for a few days.'

'Don't worry,' said Lindiwe. 'Anton will be here soon, then you can watch everything through the gate. I'll stay down here with you – I think I'd like to watch from the ground as well.'

'So will I,' said Mandy, not wanting to upset her friend.

'No. You should climb up there,' suggested James. 'Just in case we can't see everything. Then you can tell us what's going on.'

Mandy thought for a moment. It probably did make sense for someone to have a bird's-eye view. 'OK,' she said. 'I'll give you a running commentary!' She started to edge her way up the trunk of the tree. 'By the way, Lindiwe,' she called, 'Levina said we could all ride with her in the Land-rover when the giraffes get taken into the reserve. Are you coming too?'

'You bet!' said Lindiwe enthusiastically. 'I don't want to miss a thing. I've got an essay to do for school about something that happened in the holidays. I think I'll be the only one in my class to write about giraffes being released!'

As the sun grew stronger, the mist began to clear. Mandy gazed out beyond the *boma* and noticed that the pace of the bush life had started to quicken. From her perch, she could see lizards creeping out from crevices to lie on rocks in the sun's warmth. In the trees and bushes inside the *boma*, Mandy spotted tiny sunbirds, their metallic colours glinting in the morning light, probing flowers with their long, curved beaks for a breakfast of nectar.

David was the next to arrive, his camera slung round his neck. Mandy saw him before the others, and waved. When he reached the *boma*, James suggested that he join Mandy in the tree. 'You can take pictures from up there, and I'll get the ground level shots,' he said.

'Good idea,' said Adam Hope, walking up to them. 'You should end up with a pretty good record between you.'

'Don't forget I want copies of all the pictures!' said Mandy with a grin, as she watched David settling on to a branch above her. Turning back towards the *boma*, she almost fell off her branch when she found herself looking straight down into a pair of huge brown eyes. Lucky had silently sidled up to the fence and was standing just below her.

'Lucky!' she gasped. 'I didn't hear you creeping up on us!'

'It makes a change to be looking *down* at a

giraffe,' whispered David.

Very slowly, Mandy reached down so that her hand was just above Lucky's head. The calf stretched up, sniffing and blowing at Mandy's hand. She could feel little warm puffs of air as he investigated her fingers.

'I hope he doesn't sneeze!' David said softly, as he lifted his camera to take a photograph.

The quiet was broken by sound of an engine, heralding the approach of Anton and his team. Lucky pricked up his ears as the lorry drew up at the *boma*. One of the men got out and began to open the heavy gates. The rattling and clattering seemed to disturb the calf, who quickly turned and cantered back to his mother.

Anton reversed the lorry through the opening and stopped a little way into the enclosure. Mandy could see Paul, Bongani and Mduduzi unloading several large wooden panels from the back of the truck to form a funnel-shaped path leading into the back of the vehicle. Mandy knew that the plan was to herd the giraffes along the funnel and up the ramp. As the men closed the space behind them, Lucky and Chance would have no choice but to climb the ramp. It reminded Mandy of the way sheep were herded into pens by sheepdogs back home in Yorkshire.

Outside the fence, Mandy saw a Land-rover draw up. Levina and Sipho climbed out. 'We thought we'd bring the Land-rover round here to save us all walking to the garage later,' Levina told Mr and Mrs Hope, as she walked towards the gate. 'Let's go into the *boma*. You should be able to get some good photos, James.'

Mandy caught herself holding her breath as the rangers crept up behind the giraffes and began to usher them towards the funnel. She hoped that the giraffes wouldn't panic and start galloping all over the *boma*. Chance was looking a bit tense, Mandy noticed, but she continued to walk steadily in the right direction. Occasionally she would glance furtively at the men behind her but she kept going. Lucky kept close to his mother's side, his nostrils flaring and his head jerking nervously.

'Poor Lucky,' Mandy commented to David. 'He's terrified.'

The men started to walk faster as they neared the entrance to the funnel, clapping their hands from time to time. Then, walking close to each other, they formed a human barricade and steered the giraffes into the funnel.

Just where the funnel began to narrow, Chance

suddenly stopped. Lucky stopped too, hesitating as Chance gazed around, sniffing the air and peering over the side of the wooden panels. Mandy watched anxiously as the giraffe twisted her neck and looked behind her. Anton started to walk down the pathway. Chance turned, facing forwards again and broke into a slow trot, with Lucky following her. Chance reached the ramp leading into the back of the lorry, hesitated for just a moment, then walked straight up to the top.

'Phew,' said Mandy, turning to David. 'I thought for a moment they weren't going to go in.'

'So did I,' said David, grinning as he pushed his fair hair back off his face.

Lucky had also stopped at the foot of the ramp. Mandy was certain that he would follow his mother, who was standing calmly in the back of the truck. But the calf seemed to have other ideas. In one smooth movement, he swung round and began to gallop back along the pathway. The men were too late to stop Lucky dashing off, but Anton and Bongani quickly ran to the back of the lorry and pulled across a strong pole to prevent Chance from going after her calf.

Mandy looked down at James who was taking a

photograph of Anton and Bongani barricading Chance in the back of the lorry. He lowered his camera and glanced up at Mandy. Then he pointed in the direction Lucky had taken off and shrugged his shoulders. Mandy raised her hands and shrugged her shoulders too.

'Now what's going to happen?' she said grimly to David.

'It looks like Paul and Mduduzi are going to try to herd Lucky back in,' said David, leaning forward to get a better view.

The two men had begun to walk towards the calf, but Lucky managed to sidestep them and cantered into the wider area of the *boma*.

Mandy watched the calf through her binoculars. 'He's petrified!' she whispered.

David nodded. 'I suppose it's his instinct to run,' he said.

The men tried to get behind Lucky to herd him back into the funnelled pathway, but each time they drew near to him, he dodged them.

'It looks like a game of rugby,' said David, stifling a laugh.

Mandy gazed intently through her binoculars. After a few minutes, Anton went over to Paul and handed him a rope, and she thought she heard him say something about a lasso. Paul tied a large loop at one end of the rope then slowly approached the calf. Mandy could see Lucky breathing heavily. He eyed the man suspiciously and then careered away as the rope came hurtling towards him.

'This is awful,' gasped Mandy in horror. 'Lucky is never going to let them get near him.' She looked down at James. He gestured towards her and then towards the calf, and started to mouth something at her. Then suddenly it dawned on her what he was telling her. She might be able to help!

Mandy slipped down the tree and edged through the gate into the *boma* to where James and her parents were standing with Levina and Sipho. 'Levina,' she cried. 'Do you think I could have a go at getting Lucky into the lorry? I think he knows me. He might not be so frightened.'

Sipho turned to look at her and frowned. 'He's too distressed, Mandy. I don't think he will even see a difference between you and the men,' he said.

'But he *might*,' Mandy persisted. 'We've got to do something. Look! He's terrified.'

'The best we can do is to keep well out of the

way,' Mrs Hope said to Mandy. 'He *is* frightened, but we don't want to make things worse.'

'I agree,' said Mandy's father, looking serious. 'Leave it to the experts, Mandy.'

The rangers were still trying to capture the panicking calf. Lucky was beginning to look exhausted.

'But Lucky *likes* Mandy,' James said imploringly to Levina.

'One thing's certain,' said Levina, 'this can't go on much longer. The calf is already very distressed. Perhaps we *should* let Mandy try. I saw the interaction between her and the calf yesterday. There *does* seem to be a bond between them.' She turned to Sipho, 'It could be worth a shot.'

'Yes, but it could also be dangerous,' said Sipho hesitantly. 'That calf is almost crazed now.'

Levina looked at Mr and Mrs Hope questioningly. 'What do you think? Would you let Mandy go near him?'

'I suppose so,' said Adam Hope, slowly. 'If Sipho really feels it will help.'

'*Please* let me try, Sipho,' Mandy begged.

'Yes, *Baba*, please,' echoed Lindiwe.

'All right,' sighed Sipho. 'If you think it'll work, we'll try.' He stepped forward and whistled then

waved to attract Anton's attention.

Anton looked unconvinced as Sipho explained their plan. 'That calf's not going to trust anyone right now,' he protested.

'But he does seem to have taken a liking to Mandy,' Levina told him. 'He's approached her quite freely a few times. I think it's worth a shot.'

Anton agreed reluctantly to the plan and signalled to his men to leave the giraffe.

'What's up?' asked Paul, as he and Mduduzi came over to Anton.

'Mandy's taking over from us!' remarked Anton with a touch of amusement in his voice.

Anton led Mandy through the barriers towards the frightened calf, then backed away.

Lucky was standing behind one of the bare acacias near the far side of the *boma*. Mandy could see him peering at her through the stripped branches. He looked at her, blinking uncertainly as she slowly edged her way towards him. Then Mandy stopped and stood very still, giving him time to calm down and to get used to her being there. For several long minutes, neither of them moved.

Then, timidly, Lucky walked up to Mandy and began sniffing and licking her as he had before.

'Come with me, Lucky,' she whispered softly. 'Please come with me.'

Mandy began to edge slowly towards the lorry, Lucky keeping pace with her as she did so. She moved down the funnelled pathway, stopping every few steps to reassure the frightened animal.

When she reached the ramp, Mandy stopped. Bongani was standing to one side, ready to raise the ramp as soon as Lucky was inside the lorry. From the back of the vehicle, Chance gazed down at her calf. Mandy started to coax Lucky up the ramp. The calf took a few steps forward. Then, seeing his mother, he swiftly clambered up the ramp and went straight to her to suckle. Mandy sighed in relief.

'Well done, Mandy,' called Levina as Mandy moved quickly aside so that Bongani could raise the ramp.

'I think you must know the language of the giraffes,' Sipho told her, as she joined the others heading for the Land-rover.

James limped alongside her. 'I *knew* you'd do it,' he said, triumphantly.

It took about fifteen minutes to drive to the site where the giraffes were to be released. When they arrived, Anton and Bongani jumped out of the lorry and lowered the ramp at the back.

Mandy, James, Lindiwe and David waited silently in the Land-rover. Mandy watched Chance looking out over the sides of the lorry, surveying the savannah around her. Then, with her calf following, she walked down the ramp and stepped out on to the ground. The two giraffes paused for a moment, and Mandy wondered if they were trying to get their bearings. They swished their tails from side to side and their ears twitched, listening for signs of danger.

The giraffes began to move away from the lorry and headed in the direction of some tall fever trees. They stopped to browse for a minute then turned to look back at the Land-rover and the lorry.

'It's as if they're saying goodbye,' said Mandy, wistfully.

'Look,' James whispered. 'More giraffes – over there.'

In the distance, peering over the tops of some trees, a herd of giraffes was watching the progress of the newcomers. Chance had obviously seen them too. She gazed at them briefly, then started to run effortlessly towards them. Lucky broke into a graceful gallop behind his mother and the two animals moved smoothly and swiftly away, almost as if they were sailing through the bush.

From the Land-rover, Mandy watched them retreating. The operation had been a complete success. She could still see the giraffes galloping farther into the savannah, growing smaller as they went. Then, quite suddenly, they merged with their surroundings and disappeared.

'They've gone!' she said, feeling relief and sadness at the same time.

'Yes,' said Sipho. 'They are back in the bush where they belong.' He looked towards the trees where the giraffes had faded from view and quietly said, '*Hamba kahle*, Lucky. *Hamba kahle*, Chance. Go well my friends.'

'*Hamba kahle*,' echoed Mandy, as Levina started up the Land-rover and turned it to go back to the Lodge. 'Goodbye, beautiful giraffes. Stay well.'

# ANIMAL ARK *by Lucy Daniels*

| | | | |
|---|---|---|---|
| 1 | KITTENS IN THE KITCHEN | £3.99 | ❐ |
| 2 | PONY IN THE PORCH | £3.99 | ❐ |
| 3 | PUPPIES IN THE PANTRY | £3.99 | ❐ |
| 4 | GOAT IN THE GARDEN | £3.99 | ❐ |
| 5 | HEDGEHOGS IN THE HALL | £3.99 | ❐ |
| 6 | BADGER IN THE BASEMENT | £3.99 | ❐ |
| 7 | CUB IN THE CUPBOARD | £3.99 | ❐ |
| 8 | PIGLET IN A PLAYPEN | £3.99 | ❐ |
| 9 | OWL IN THE OFFICE | £3.99 | ❐ |
| 10 | LAMB IN THE LAUNDRY | £3.99 | ❐ |
| 11 | BUNNIES IN THE BATHROOM | £3.99 | ❐ |
| 12 | DONKEY ON THE DOORSTEP | £3.99 | ❐ |
| 13 | HAMSTER IN A HAMPER | £3.99 | ❐ |
| 14 | GOOSE ON THE LOOSE | £3.99 | ❐ |
| 15 | CALF IN THE COTTAGE | £3.99 | ❐ |
| 16 | KOALA IN A CRISIS | £3.99 | ❐ |
| 17 | WOMBAT IN THE WILD | £3.99 | ❐ |
| 18 | ROO ON THE ROCK | £3.99 | ❐ |
| 19 | SQUIRRELS IN THE SCHOOL | £3.99 | ❐ |
| 20 | GUINEA-PIG IN THE GARAGE | £3.99 | ❐ |
| 21 | FAWN IN THE FOREST | £3.99 | ❐ |
| 22 | SHETLAND IN THE SHED | £3.99 | ❐ |
| 23 | SWAN IN THE SWIM | £3.99 | ❐ |
| 24 | LION BY THE LAKE | £3.99 | ❐ |
| 25 | ELEPHANTS IN THE EAST | £3.99 | ❐ |
| 26 | MONKEYS ON THE MOUNTAIN | £3.99 | ❐ |
| 27 | DOG AT THE DOOR | £3.99 | ❐ |
| 28 | FOALS IN THE FIELD | £3.99 | ❐ |
| 29 | SHEEP AT THE SHOW | £3.99 | ❐ |
| 30 | RACOONS ON THE ROOF | £3.99 | ❐ |
| 31 | DOLPHIN IN THE DEEP | £3.99 | ❐ |
| 32 | BEARS IN THE BARN | £3.99 | ❐ |
| 33 | OTTER IN THE OUTHOUSE | £3.99 | ❐ |
| 34 | WHALE IN THE WAVES | £3.99 | ❐ |
| 35 | HOUND AT THE HOSPITAL | £3.99 | ❐ |
| 36 | RABBITS ON THE RUN | £3.99 | ❐ |
| 37 | HORSE IN THE HOUSE | £3.99 | ❐ |
| 38 | PANDA IN THE PARK | £3.99 | ❐ |
| 39 | TIGER ON THE TRACK | £3.99 | ❐ |
| 40 | GORILLA IN THE GLADE | £3.99 | ❐ |
| 41 | TABBY IN THE TUB | £3.99 | ❐ |
| 42 | CHINCHILLA UP THE CHIMNEY | £3.99 | ❐ |
| 43 | PUPPY IN A PUDDLE | £3.99 | ❐ |
| 44 | LEOPARD AT THE LODGE | £3.99 | ❐ |
| | SHEEPDOG IN THE SNOW | £3.99 | ❐ |
| | KITTEN IN THE COLD | £3.99 | ❐ |
| | FOX IN THE FROST | £3.99 | ❐ |
| | HAMSTER IN THE HOLLY | £3.99 | ❐ |
| | PONY IN THE POST | £3.99 | ❐ |
| | PONIES AT THE POINT | £3.99 | ❐ |
| | SEAL ON THE SHORE | £3.99 | ❐ |
| | ANIMAL ARK FAVOURITES | £3.99 | ❐ |
| | PIGS AT THE PICNIC | £3.99 | ❐ |
| | DOG IN THE DUNGEON | £3.99 | ❐ |
| | CAT IN THE CRYPT | £3.99 | ❐ |
| | STALLION IN THE STORM | £3.99 | ❐ |
| | PONY IN THE POST | £3.99 | ❐ |
| | WILDLIFE WAYS | £9.99 | ❐ |

*All Hodder Children's books are available at your local bookshop, or can be ordered direct from the publisher. Just tick the titles you would like and complete the details below. Prices and availability are subject to change without prior notice.*

Please enclose a cheque or postal order made payable to *Bookpoint Ltd*, and send to: Hodder Children's Books, 39 Milton Park, Abingdon, OXON OX14 4TD, UK. Email Address: orders@bookpoint.co.uk

If you would prefer to pay by credit card, our call centre team would be delighted to take your order by telephone. Our direct line *01235 400414* (lines open 9.00 am–6.00 pm Monday to Saturday, 24 hour message answering service). Alternatively you can send a fax on *01235 400454*.

| TITLE | | FIRST NAME | | SURNAME | |
|---|---|---|---|---|---|

| ADDRESS | |
|---|---|
| | |
| | |
| DAYTIME TEL: | | POST CODE | |

If you would prefer to pay by credit card, please complete:
Please debit my Visa/Access/Diner's Card/American Express (delete as applicable) card no:

| | | | | | | | | | | | | | | | | | |
|---|---|---|---|---|---|---|---|---|---|---|---|---|---|---|---|---|---|

Signature ..............................................................................

Expiry Date: .......................................................................

If you would NOT like to receive further information on our products please tick the box. ❐